Paddington Goes to Town

Paddington Goes to Town

MICHAEL BOND

Illustrations by Peggy Fortnum

A YEARLING BOOK

Published by
DELL PUBLISHING CO., INC.
1 Dag Hammarskjold Plaza
New York, N.Y. 10017
Copyright © 1968 by Michael Bond
ISBN: 0-440-46793-4
For information address Houghton Mifflin Company,
Boston, Massachusetts 02107.
Reprinted by arrangement with Houghton Mifflin Company
Printed in the United States of America
Eighth Dell Printing—April 1979

CW

CONTENTS

CHAPTER ONE

A Day to Remember

Mrs. Brown stared at Paddington in amazement. "Harold Price wants you to be an usher at his wedding?" she repeated. "Are you sure?"

Paddington nodded. "I've just met him in the market, Mrs. Brown," he explained. "He said he was going to give you a ring as well."

Mrs. Brown exchanged glances with the rest of the family as they gathered round to hear Paddington's news.

Harold Price was a young man who served on the preserves counter at a large grocery store in the Portobello Road, and the events leading up to his forthcoming marriage to Miss Deirdre Flint, who worked on the adjacent bacon and eggs counter, had been watched with interest by the Browns, particularly as it was largely through Paddington that they had become engaged in the first place.

It had all come about some months previously when Paddington had lent a paw at a local drama festival in which Miss Flint had played the lead in one of Mr. Price's plays.

A great many things had gone wrong that evening, but Mr. Price always maintained afterwards that far from Paddington causing a parting of the ways, he and Miss Flint had been brought even closer together. At any event, shortly afterwards they had announced their engagement.

It was largely because of Paddington's part in the affair, and the numerous large orders for marmalade he'd placed with Mr. Price over the years, that all the Browns had been invited to the wedding that day; but never in their wildest dreams had it occurred to any of them that Paddington might be one of the officials.

During the silence which followed while everyone considered the matter, he held up a small, bright metal object. "Mr. Price has given me the key to his flat," he announced importantly. "He wants me to pick up the list of guests on the way to the church."

"Well, I must say it's rather a nice idea," said Mrs. Brown, trying to sound more enthusiastic than she actually felt. "It's really a case of history repeating itself."

"Remembering what happened last time," murmured Mr. Brown, "I only hope it doesn't repeat itself too faithfully."

"Everything turned out all right in the end," Mrs. Brown broke in hastily, as Paddington gave one of his hard stares. "Harold's play *did* win first prize and he was very glad of Paddington's help when the sound effects man let him down."

"I think he's been let down again, Mrs. Brown," said Paddington earnestly. "He's got no one to keep quiet during the ceremony."

"No one to keep quiet?" echoed Jonathan. Paddington's thought processes were sometimes rather difficult to follow, and his present one was no exception.

"I've no doubt that bear will do as well as anyone if he sets his mind to it," said Mrs. Bird, the Browns' housekeeper, as Paddington, having startled everybody by announcing that he was going to have a special bath in honour of the occasion, disappeared upstairs in order to carry out his threat. "No doubt at all. After all, it's only a matter of lending a paw and showing people to their right places in the church."

"Knowing the usual state of Paddington's paws," replied Mr. Brown, "I think I'd sooner find my own way."

"He *is* having a bath, Daddy," reminded Judy. "He's just said so."

"He may be having a bath," retorted Mr. Brown grimly. "But he's still got to get to the church. All sorts of things can happen before then."

"'Ush!" cried Jonathan suddenly. "I bet he thinks being an Usher means he has to keep 'ush during the service."

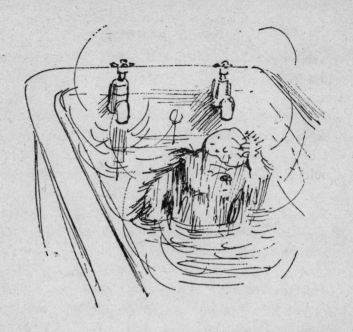

"Oh, dear," said Mrs. Brown, as Jonathan's words sank in. "I do hope he doesn't tell Deirdre to be quiet when she's making her responses. You know what a quick temper she's got and I expect she'll be all on edge as it is."

Mrs. Brown began to look somewhat less happy about the whole affair as she turned the matter over in her mind, but at that moment the shrill sound of the telephone bell broke into her thoughts.

"It's Harold Price," she hissed, putting her hand over the receiver. "He wants to know if it's all right. What *shall* I say?"

Mr. Brown looked up at the ceiling as the sound of running water came from somewhere overhead. "Whatever we say it had better not be 'no'," he replied. "Not at this stage. We shall never hear the last of it if Paddington's had a bath for nothing. Especially one he's volunteered for.

"All the same," he continued, giving his suit a passing flick with the clothes-brush, "I can't help feeling it isn't the best of ways to start married life. I don't think I should have been very keen on having a bear as an usher at my wedding – even if I had been let down."

Mr. Brown wasn't over enthusiastic about weddings at the best of times, and the thought of attending one at which Paddington was lending a paw filled him with foreboding.

Nevertheless, even Mr. Brown's fears were gradually set at rest as the day wore on, for Paddington's behaviour seemed beyond reproach.

When they arrived at the church he was busily engaged with a long and important-looking list of names which enabled him to check the invitations and sort out the friends of the bride from those of the groom, and as he led them down the aisle towards their allotted places they couldn't help noticing how spick and span he looked. His fur had a newly-brushed, glistening appearance, and his whiskers were so shiny they made the large white carnation which he wore tied round his neck look almost dowdy by comparison.

If the Browns had any criticism at all it was that he was taking his job a little over seriously. Jonathan's earlier theory proved all too correct and as soon as anyone so much as parted their lips he hurried up to them with his paw raised and gave them a hard stare. Some of his stares, which had been handed down to him by his Aunt Lucy in Peru, were very powerful indeed and in no time at all it would have been possible to have heard the proverbial pin drop.

Even the vicar looked most impressed when he came into the church and saw the attentive state of his congregation.

"I don't see how we *can* explain now," hissed Mr. Brown. "It's a bit difficult when you're not allowed to say anything."

The others contented themselves with a nod of agreement, for at that moment Paddington, having carefully checked the list of guests for the last time to make certain everyone was present, settled himself down in a nearby pew in order to consult his programme and enjoy the forthcoming ceremony in comfort.

In any case, they soon had other matters to occupy their minds for a moment or so later Mr. Price and his best man arrived and took up their places near the front.

They both looked unusually agitated, even for such a nerve-racking occasion as a wedding, and Mr. Price in particular kept jumping up and down like a jack-in-the-box. He seemed to want to speak to Paddington, but each time he turned round and opened his mouth Paddington put a paw firmly to his lips.

"I don't remember Harold having that nervous twitch before," whispered Mrs. Brown, uneasily.

"I think it's got something to do with the ring,"

whispered Judy, passing on what little bit of information she'd been able to glean from those in front. "They're having to make do with a brass one off Mr. Price's bedroom curtains. Apparently the real one's disappeared."

"Disappeared!" echoed Mrs. Brown. For a moment she quite forgot Paddington's presence in the nearby pew, but as it happened she needn't have worried, for Paddington seemed even more affected than anyone by this latest piece of news. His whiskers sagged, his face took on a sudden woebegone expression, and even the carnation round his neck seemed to wilt in sympathy.

"Deirdre's not going to be very pleased when she hears," murmured Mr. Brown. "I shouldn't like to be the person who's got it!"

"Ssh!" hissed Mrs. Brown. "Here she comes!"

The Browns fell silent as there was a rustle of silk behind them and Deirdre, resplendent in a snow-white wedding gown, sailed past on the arm of Mr. Flint.

Only Paddington failed to join in the general gasps of admiration which greeted her entrance. For some reason best known to himself he appeared to be engaged in a kind of life and death struggle on the floor of the church. Several times he was lost to view completely and each time he rose again he was breathing more and more heavily and his expression looked, if possible, unhappier than before.

However, unhappy though it was, it seemed almost gay by comparison with the grim one which came over Miss Flint's face a moment or so later when she took in the whispered aside from her husband-to-be.

For one brief moment indeed, it looked as if for two pins Miss Flint would have called the whole thing off, and when it came to the time for her to say "I do", there was quite a nasty pause before she managed to get the words out.

When the ceremony finally came to an end both she and Harold hurried towards the vestry in order to sign the register rather as if they had a bus to catch, and not a bit like two people who had just agreed to spend the rest of their lives together.

"I'm glad I'm not in Harold's shoes," said Mr. Brown, as the door closed behind them. "Deirdre looked as black as thunder."

"Ssh!" began Mrs. Brown. "We don't want Pad . . ."

She was about to say that one upset was enough and they didn't want to add to the confusion by having Paddington take up his 'ushing duties again, but as she looked round the church it was only to discover that Paddington was nowhere in sight.

"There he is!" cried Judy suddenly, as she looked back over her shoulder.

Turning round to follow her gaze the rest of the Browns were just in time to catch a glimpse of a familiar figure hurrying up the aisle in the direction of the entrance doors.

"Perhaps he wants to be in the front of the photograph," said Mrs. Brown hopefully, as Paddington, after casting an anxious glance over his shoulder, picked up his

suitcase and hat from behind a nearby pillar and disappeared from view. "He's always very keen on anything
like that for his scrap-book, and he looks as if he's got
something on his mind."

"Hmm," said Mrs. Bird. "That's as may be. But if you
ask me that young bear's mind is not the only thing he's
got something on."

Mrs. Bird's sharp eyes had noticed a momentary gleam
from one of Paddington's paws as he'd gone out into the
sunshine. It was the second time within the space of a few
minutes she'd spotted the strange phenomenon. The first
occasion had been during the service itself, when the vicar
had asked the assembly if anyone present knew of any

good reason why Deirdre and Harold shouldn't get married. Paddington had half raised his paw and then, much to her relief, he'd changed his mind at the last moment.

Mrs. Bird was good at adding two and two together as far as Paddington was concerned, but wisely she kept the result of her calculations to herself for the time being.

In any case, before the others had time to question her on the subject a rather worried looking churchwarden hurried up the aisle and stopped at their pew in order to whisper something in Mr. Brown's ear.

Mr. Brown rose to his feet. "I think we're wanted in the vestry," he announced ominously. "It sounds rather urgent."

Mr. Brown was tempted to add that the churchwarden had also asked if Paddington could accompany them, but in the event he decided not to add to their worries.

All the same, as he led the way into the vestry he began to look more and more worried, and if he'd been able to see through the stone walls into the churchyard outside the chances are that he would have felt even more so.

For Paddington was in trouble. Quite serious trouble. One way and another he was used to life having its ups and downs, but as he held his paw up to the light in order to examine it more closely even he had to admit he couldn't remember a time when his fortunes had taken quite such a downward plunge.

Sucking it had made no difference at all; jamming it in the railings which surrounded the churchyard only seemed to have made matters worse; and even the application of a liberal smear of marmalade from an emergency jar which he kept in his suitcase had been to no avail.

As far as paws went, his own was looking unusually smart and well cared for. Apart from the remains of the marmalade it wouldn't have disgraced an advertisement for fur coats in one of Mrs. Brown's glossy magazines. Even the pad had an unusual glow about it, not unlike that of a newly polished shoe.

However, it wasn't the pad or its surroundings which caused Paddington's look of dismay, but the sight of a small gold wedding-ring poking out from beneath his fur; and the longer he looked at it the more unhappy he became.

He'd found the ring lying on the dressing-table when he'd gone to Harold Price's room in order to pick up the wedding list, and at the time it had gone on one of his claws easily enough. But now it was well and truly stuck, and nothing he could do would make it budge one way or the other.

In the past he had always kept on very good terms with Mr. Price. Even so, he couldn't begin to imagine what his friend would have to say about the matter. Nor, when he considered it, could he picture Deirdre exactly laughing her head off when she heard the news that her wedding-ring was stuck round a bend on a bear's paw. From past experience he knew that Deirdre had a very sharp tongue indeed when even quite minor things went wrong with her bacon-slicer, and he shuddered to think what she would have to say about the present situation.

As if to prove how right he was, his thoughts were

broken into at that very moment, as the sound of Deirdre's voice raised in anger floated out through the open window above his head.

By climbing on top of his suitcase and standing on tip-toe Paddington was just able to see inside the vestry and when he did so he nearly fell over backwards again in alarm, for not only was Deirdre there, laying down the law to a most unhappy-looking Mr. Price; but the best man, sundry relatives, the Browns and quite a number of other important-looking people were there as well.

Indeed, so great was the crowd and so loud the argument, it gave the impression that more people were attending the signing of the register than had been present at the actual ceremony.

Paddington was a hopeful bear at heart but the more he listened to Deirdre the more his spirits dropped and the more he realised the only thing they had in common was a wish that he'd never been invited to the wedding in the first place, let alone act as an usher.

After a moment or two he clambered back down again, took a deep breath, picked up his suitcase and headed towards a large red box just outside the churchyard.

It wasn't often that Paddington made a telephone call — for one thing he always found it a bit difficult with paws — but he did remember once reading a poster in a phone box about what to do in times of an emergency and how it was possible to obtain help without paying.

It had seemed very good value at the time and as far as he could make out it would be difficult to think of a

situation which was more of an emergency than his present one.

His brief appearance at the window didn't go entirely unnoticed, but fortunately the only person who saw him was Judy, and by the time she'd passed the message on to Jonathan he'd disappeared again.

"Perhaps it was a mirage," said Jonathan hopefully.

"It wasn't," said Judy. "It was Paddington's hat."

"Paddington!" echoed Deirdre, catching the end of Judy's reply. "Don't mention that name to me."

"Look!" she announced dramatically, holding up her wedding finger for what seemed to her audience like the hundredth time. "A curtain ring! A brass curtain ring!"

"I thought it would be better than nothing," said the best man, hastily cupping his hands under Deirdre's in

case the object of her wrath fell off. "I was hoping you
might have big fingers."

Deirdre gave the best man a withering glare and then
turned her attention back to the unfortunate Harold.
"Don't just stand there," she exclaimed. "*Do* something!"

"Look here," broke in Mr. Brown. "I still don't see
why you're blaming Paddington."

"My room's on the fifth floor," said Mr. Price, briefly.
"And there are only two keys. Paddington had the other
one."

"Fancy asking a bear to be an usher," said Deirdre,
scornfully. "You might have known *something* would happen. I shall never be able to show my face in the shop again.
Practically all our best customers are here."

The new Mrs. Price broke off as quite clearly above her
words there came the sound of a fire-bell, at first in the
distance, and then gradually getting closer and closer.

The vicar glanced nervously out of his vestry window.
Quite a crowd seemed to have collected outside the church
and even as he watched, a large, red fire-engine, its bell
clanging furiously, screamed to a halt and several men in
blue uniform jumped off, their hatchets at the ready.

"That's all I need," said Deirdre bitterly, as the vicar
excused himself and hurried off to investigate the matter.
"A fire! That'll round off the day nicely!"

The room fell silent as Mr. Price's bride, having
exhausted the topic of the things she would like to do,
embarked on a long list of the things she *wasn't* going to
do under any circumstances until she got her wedding-

ring back; including signing the register, having her photograph taken, and going on her honeymoon.

It was just as she reached the last item, and Mr. Price's face had fallen to its longest ever, that the door burst open and the vicar hurried back into the room closely followed by a man in fireman's uniform, and behind him, Paddington himself.

"*There* you are, Paddington," said Mrs. Brown thankfully. "*Where* have you been?"

"Having a bit of a sticky time of it, if you ask me, ma'am," began the fireman, "what with one thing and another."

"My ring!" broke in Deirdre, catching sight of a shiny object in Paddington's outstretched paw.

"I'm afraid it got stuck round a bend, Mrs. Price," explained Paddington.

"Stuck round a *bend*?" repeated Deirdre disbelievingly. "How on earth did that happen?"

Paddington took hold of the ring in his other paw in order to demonstrate exactly what had gone wrong. "I'm not sure," he admitted truthfully. "I just slipped it on for safety and when I tried to take it off again . . ."

The fireman gave a groan. "Don't say you've done it again!" he exclaimed. "I've only just got it off."

"Bears!" groaned Deirdre. "I'm not meant to get married."

"What I can't understand," said Mr. Price, "is why you put it on your paw in the first place, Mr. Brown."

"You said you were going to give Mrs. Brown a ring," said Paddington unhappily. "I thought I'd save you the bother."

"I said I was going to give Mrs. Brown a ring?" repeated Harold, hardly able to believe his ears.

"I think you did," said Mrs. Brown. "Paddington probably didn't realise you meant a ring on the telephone."

"Quite a natural mistake," said Mrs. Bird in the silence which followed. "Anyone might have made it in the circumstances."

"Never mind," said the fireman. "What goes on must come off — especially the second time."

"I tell you what," he continued, sizing up the situation as he got to work on Paddington's paw with a pair of pliers, "if the happy couple would like to sign the register while I do this, I'll get my crew to form a guard of honour outside the church."

"A guard of honour!" exclaimed Deirdre.

"With axes," said the fireman.

The new Mrs. Price began to look slightly better pleased. "Well, I don't know really . . ." she simpered, patting her hair.

"It's a bit irregular," whispered the fireman in Paddington's ear, "and we don't normally do it for people outside the service, but we've a big recruiting drive on at the moment and it'll be good publicity. Besides, it'll help calm things down a bit."

"Thank you very much," said Paddington gratefully. "I shall ask for you if ever I have a real fire."

"It'll make a lovely photograph," said Harold persuasively, taking Deirdre's hand and leading her across the room. "And it'll be something to show the girls back in the shop."

"If the ring won't come off, perhaps I could come on the honeymoon with you, Mrs. Price," said Paddington hopefully. "I've never been on one of those before."

Deirdre's back stiffened as she bent down to sign the register.

"I don't think that'll be necessary," said the fireman hastily, as he removed the ring at long last and handed it to Mr. Price for safe keeping.

23

"Tell you what, though," he added, seeing a look of disappointment cross Paddington's face. "As you can't go on the honeymoon perhaps we'll give you a lift to the wedding breakfast on our way back to the station instead.

"After all," he continued, looking meaningly at Mrs. Price, "if this young bear hadn't had the good sense to call us when he did he might still be wearing the ring and then where would you be?"

And to that remark not even Deirdre could find an answer.

"Gosh!" said Jonathan, as the Browns made their way back up the aisle. "Fancy riding on the back of a fire-engine!"

"I don't suppose there are many bears who can say they've done that," agreed Judy.

Paddington nodded. A lot of things seemed about to happen all at once, and he wasn't quite sure which he was looking forward to most. Apart from the promised ride he'd never heard of anyone having their breakfast in the afternoon before, let alone a wedding one, but it sounded a very good way of rounding things off.

"If you and Mrs. Price ever want to get married again," he announced, as Harold led Deirdre out of the church and paused for the photographers beneath an archway of raised fire axes, "I'll do some more 'ushing for you if you like."

Deirdre shuddered. "Never again," she said, taking a firm grip on Harold's arm. "Once is quite enough."

Mr. Price nodded his agreement. "It's as I said in the

beginning," he remarked, from beneath a shower of confetti, "young Mr. Brown has a habit of bringing people closer together in the end, and this time it's for good!"

CHAPTER TWO

Paddington Hits Out

"I know it's none of my business," said Mrs. Bird, pausing for a moment as she cleared the breakfast table, "but do you think Mr. Curry's suddenly come into some money?" She nodded towards the next-door garden. "He's out there practising with his golf clubs again this morning. That's the third time this week."

"I must say it's very strange," agreed Mrs. Brown, as the clear sound of a ball being hit by a club greeted her housekeeper's remarks. "He seemed to be turning his lawn into a putting green yesterday and he's got some plus-fours hanging on the line."

Paddington, who until that moment had been busily

26

engaged in finishing up the last of the toast and marmalade before Mrs. Bird removed it from the table, suddenly
gave vent to a loud choking noise. "Mr. Curry's plus-fours
are hanging on the line!" he exclaimed when he had
recovered himself.

He peered through the window with interest, but Mr.
Curry's clothes line seemed very little different from any
other day of the week. In fact, apart from a tea towel and
jerseys the only unusual item was a pair of very odd-
looking trousers which hung limp and bedraggled in the
still morning air.

"Those *are* plus-fours," explained Mrs. Brown.
"They're special trousers people used to wear when they
played golf. You don't often see them nowadays."

Mrs. Brown looked just as puzzled as her housekeeper
as she considered Mr. Curry's strange behaviour. Apart
from having a reputation for meanness, the Brown's neighbour was also noted for his bad temper and unsportsman-
like attitude generally. The idea of his taking up any sort
of game was hard to picture and when it was an expensive
one like golf then it became doubly so.

"That reminds me," she continued, turning away from
the window. "Henry asked me to get *his* golfing things
out for him. There's an 'open day' at the golf club on
Saturday and he wants to go. They're expecting quite a
crowd. Arnold Parker's putting in a special appearance
and he's judging one or two competitions. I don't know
whether Henry's going in for any of them but apparently
there are some quite big prizes. There's a special one

for the person whose ball travels the farthest and . . ."

"Hmm," said Mrs. Bird as Mrs. Brown's voice trailed away. "There's no need to say any more. That's one mystery solved!"

Although she wasn't in the habit of interesting herself in other people's affairs Mrs. Bird liked to get to the bottom of things. "Trust Mr. Curry to be around when there's a chance of getting something for nothing," she snorted as she disappeared towards the kitchen with her tray.

As Mrs. Brown picked up the remains of the crockery and followed her housekeeper out of the room Paddington climbed up on to his chair and looked hopefully out of the window. But Mr. Curry was nowhere in sight and even the sound of shots being practised seemed to have died away, so he climbed back down again and a few minutes later hurried out into the garden in order to investigate the matter more closely.

In the past he'd several times come across Mr. Brown's golf clubs in the cupboard under the stairs, but he'd never watched the game being played before and the possibility of seeing Mr. Curry practising on his lawn and being able to take a closer look at his plus-fours into the bargain seemed an opportunity too good to be missed.

Crouching down to the ground behind Mr. Brown's shed he put his eye to a special knot-hole in the fence which usually gave a very good view of the next-door garden, but to his surprise there was nothing to be seen but a wall of blackness.

Looking most disappointed Paddington picked up one of Mr. Brown's old bean sticks and poked it hopefully through the hole in an attempt to unblock it. As he did so a loud cry of pain suddenly rang out and he nearly fell over backwards with surprise as the familiar figure of the Browns' neighbour suddenly rose into view on the other side of the fence.

"Bear!" roared Mr. Curry as he danced up and down clutching his right eye. "Did you do that on purpose, bear?"

Hastily letting go of the stick Paddington jumped back in alarm. "Oh, no, Mr. Curry," he exclaimed. "I was only trying to unblock the hole. If I'd known you were there I'd have done it much more gently. I mean . . ."

"What's that?" bellowed Mr. Curry. "What did you say?"

Paddington gave up trying to explain what he meant as the face on the other side of the fence turned a deep purple.

"I wanted to see your sum trousers, Mr. Curry," he said unhappily.

"My *what* trousers?" repeated Mr. Curry.

"Your sum trousers, Mr. Curry," said Paddington. "The ones you play golf in."

Mr. Curry gave Paddington a searching look with his good eye. "If you mean my plus-fours why don't you say so, bear," he growled. Removing his hand from the other eye he glared suspiciously across the fence. "I was looking for my golf ball. It went over into your garden."

Anxious to make amends Paddington looked around

Mr. Brown's garden and almost immediately spied a small white object nestling amongst the tomato plants. "Here it is, Mr. Curry," he called. "I think it's broken one of Mr. Brown's stems."

"If people don't take the trouble to build their fences high enough they must expect these things," said Mr. Curry nastily as he took the ball.

He examined it carefully to make sure it wasn't damaged and then looked thoughtfully at Paddington. "I didn't realise you were interested in golf, bear," he remarked casually.

Paddington returned his gaze doubtfully. "I'm not sure if I am yet, Mr. Curry," he said carefully.

On more than one occasion in the past he'd been caught napping by a casual remark from the Browns' neighbour and had no wish to find himself agreeing by mistake to build a golf course for sixpence.

Mr. Curry looked over his shoulder in order to make sure no one else was around and then he signalled Paddington to come closer. "I'm looking for someone to act as caddie for me in the golf competition tomorrow," he said, lowering his voice. "I have some very expensive equipment and I need someone reliable to take charge of it all.

"If I find the right person," he continued meaningly, "I might not report whoever it is for nearly poking my eye out with a stick."

"Thank you very much, Mr. Curry," began Paddington even more doubtfully.

Almost before the words were out of his mouth Mr.

Curry rubbed his hands together. "Good! That's settled then," he said briskly. "I'll see you on the links at two o'clock sharp.

"Mind you," he added sternly as he turned to go. "If I let you do it I shall hold you responsible for *everything*. If any of my balls get lost you'll have to buy me some new ones."

Paddington stared unhappily after the retreating figure in the next-door garden. He wasn't at all sure what duties a caddie had on a golf course but from the tone of Mr. Curry's last remarks he had a nasty feeling that not for the first time he was getting the worst of the bargain.

In the event his worst fears were realised and any ideas he might have entertained of actually having a go himself were quickly dashed the following day when he met Mr. Curry at the entrance to the golf course.

The Browns' neighbour wasn't in a very good mood, and as the afternoon wore on and Paddington laboured wearily up hill and down dale, struggling with the bag of clubs, his hopes grew fainter still.

Mr. Curry seemed to spend most of his time climbing in and out of one or other of the many bunkers scattered about the eighteen holes on the golf course, his temper getting shorter and shorter, and Paddington was thankful when at long last the spot where the big competition of the day was being held came into view and they stood awaiting their turn at the start.

"You'll have to keep your eyes skinned here, bear," growled Mr. Curry, surveying the fairway. "I shall be hitting the ball very hard and you mustn't lose sight of it.

I don't want it getting mixed up with anyone else's."

"It's all right, Mr. Curry," said Paddington eagerly. "I've put a special mark on the side with some marmalade peel."

"Marmalade peel?" echoed Mr. Curry. "Are you sure it won't come off?"

"I don't think so, Mr. Curry," replied Paddington confidently. "It's some of my special marmalade from the cut-price grocers in the market. Mrs. Bird always says their chunks *never* come off anything."

Paddington glanced around while he was explaining what he'd done. Quite a large crowd had assembled to watch the event and he felt most important as he leaned nonchalantly on Mr. Curry's club in the way that he'd

seen Arnold Parker do in some of the many posters advertising the event.

Even Mr. Curry himself began to look slightly better pleased with things in general as he took in the scene around them.

"Of course, bear," he announced in a loud voice for the benefit of some near-by spectators, "I've only been practising so far. Getting my hand in so to speak. It's a long time since I played golf so I've been saving myself for this event. Now, when I go up to get my prize I'd like you to . . ."

Mr. Curry's voice broke off and whatever else he'd been about to say was lost for posterity as a loud crack rent the air and Paddington suddenly rolled over on to the grass clutching a short length of stick in his paw.

"Bear!" bellowed Mr. Curry. For once words deserted him as he pointed a trembling finger at the broken end of his golf club.

Paddington sat up and peered unhappily at the two jagged pieces. "Perhaps you could tie them together, Mr. Curry," he said hopefully.

"Tie them together!" spluttered Mr. Curry. "Tie them together! My best driver! I'll . . . I'll . . ."

"Look here," a voice at Mr. Curry's elbow broke into the argument. "If anyone is owed an apology it's this young bear. From the way you were playing earlier on I'm not surprised that club snapped. It's a wonder there wasn't a nasty accident. And if this is your best one I must say I wouldn't care to see your worst. It's all rusty!"

The owner of the voice looked distastefully at the remains of Mr. Curry's club and then bent down to give Paddington a hand. "My name's Parker," he announced. "Arnold Parker. I'm acting as judge here this afternoon."

"Thank you very much, Mr. Parker," said Paddington, looking most impressed at having such a famous person help him to his feet. "My name's Brown. Paddington Brown."

"Arnold Parker?" repeated Mr. Curry. The cross expression on his face disappeared as if by magic. "I was only joking," he said, creasing his face into a smile as he reached into his golf bag. "These things happen. I *do* have another driver. It's a much heavier one, of course . . . I really only keep it for when I'm playing in important matches . . . but still . . .

"Remind me to give you sixpence when we get home, bear," he added in a loud voice for the benefit of Arnold Parker.

Paddington blinked at the Browns' neighbour in amazement. It was most unlike him to want to pay out sixpence at the end of a hard day's work let alone offer one without so much as being asked.

"Do you happen to have my tee handy, bear?" asked Mr. Curry, as he took up his position at the start.

"Your *tea*, Mr. Curry?" repeated Paddington. Taken even more by surprise at this sudden request, he reached hastily under his hat in an effort to make amends for his accident, and withdrew a marmalade sandwich.

Mr. Curry took the sandwich, looked at it for a moment

34

as if he could hardly believe his eyes, and then threw it on the ground. "I don't mean *that* sort of tea, bear," he growled, his smile becoming even more fixed than before. "I mean the kind you place the ball on."

Taking a deep breath he reached into his pocket and withdrew a small object made of yellow plastic which he pushed into the ground in front of him.

Balancing Paddington's specially marked ball on top of the tee, Mr. Curry stood back, took careful aim along the fairway, swung the new club over his shoulder, and then to everyone's surprise gave a loud yell as in one continuous movement he turned head over heels like a catherine wheel.

"Oh, dear," said Arnold Parker. He bent down and examined something on the ground. "I think you must have accidentally trodden on Mr. Brown's marmalade sandwich!"

The golf club was situated close to a railway line and fortunately for the ears of the onlookers in general, and Paddington in particular, Mr. Curry's remarks for the next few minutes as he sat digesting this piece of information were drowned by the noise of a passing train.

"Marmalade!" he exclaimed. 'All over my best plus-fours!" He sat up rubbing his leg. "*And* I've hurt myself," he groaned. "Now I shan't be able to play."

Arnold Parker began to look rather concerned as Mr. Curry screwed up his face. "If I were you I'd go along to the First Aid tent," he said. "It may be serious."

"Bear!" roared Mr. Curry. "It's all your fault, bear.

Leaving marmalade sandwiches lying around like that."

"Nonsense!" said Arnold Parker, coming to Paddington's rescue again. "If you hadn't thrown it down in the first place it would never have happened. It's a judgement."

"Perhaps *I* could have a go for you, Mr. Curry," said Paddington eagerly.

Arnold Parker looked at him thoughtfully. "There's no reason why not," he said, turning to Mr. Curry. "It doesn't say anything in the rules about bears being barred and it'll save you losing your entrance money."

Mr. Curry pricked up his ears at this last piece of information. He glared at Paddington and then, swallowing hard, handed over his club. "All right, bear," he said, ungraciously. "I suppose it's better than nothing. But mind you make a good job of it.

"And make sure you address the ball properly," he barked, as Paddington took up his position.

"Make sure I address the ball properly, Mr. Curry?" exclaimed Paddington, looking most surprised. "I don't even know where it's going!"

"I think he's worried about your stance, Mr. Brown," said Arnold Parker soothingly.

"My *stamps*?" echoed Paddington, growing more and more confused. Looking at Mr. Curry's ball there didn't seem much room for even a short address let alone a stamp as well and he was most relieved when Arnold Parker explained that addressing the ball was only another way of saying you were getting ready to hit it and that "stance" simply described the way you stood.

Paddington looked round at the crowd. It seemed to him that golfers used a lot of very long and complicated words to describe the simple act of hitting a small white ball with a club.

Taking hold of Mr. Curry's club he closed his eyes, and to the accompaniment of a gasp of alarm from some of the nearby spectators, swung the club with all his might.

"Er . . . perhaps you could try standing a little nearer," said Arnold Parker, after a few minutes and quite a number of goes had passed by without anything happening. He looked at his watch and then at the queue of waiting competitors. "It must be a bit difficult with paws," he added encouragingly.

Paddington mopped his brow and stared at the ball in disgust. He felt there were several improvements he could make to the game of golf, not the least of which would be to have a bigger ball. All the same he was a determined bear and after deciding to have one last try he closed his eyes again, gripped the club as hard as he could, and took a final swing.

This time there was a satisfying crack as the end of the club made contact with the ball.

"Fore!" shouted someone in the crowd behind him.

"Five!" exclaimed Paddington, nearly falling over in his excitement.

"Congratulations!" said Arnold Parker, as he picked himself up off the ground. "Did anyone see where it went?"

"I did," shouted Mr. Curry above the noise of a passing goods train. "Over there!" He pointed towards a large patch of scrubland between the tee and the railway line and then turned back to Paddington.

"Bear," he said slowly and carefully, "I'm going to the First Aid tent now to get my leg seen to. If you haven't found my ball by the time I get back . . . I'll . . . I'll . . ." The Browns' neighbour left his sentence unfinished as he hobbled away, but the expression on his face more than made up for any lack of words and Paddington's heart sank as he bade good-bye to Arnold Parker and made his way slowly in the direction of the railway line.

From a distance the piece of land had looked bad enough, full of long grass and brambles, but now that he was close to it Paddington decided he wouldn't fancy his chances of finding a football let alone anything as small as a golf ball, and even the friendly sight of the train driver waving in his direction as the engine disappeared round a bend failed to cheer him up as he settled down to his unwelcome task.

Mr. Curry sat up in bed in the Casualty Ward of the hospital and stared in amazement at the shiny new bag of golf clubs. "Do you mean to say *I* won these?" he said.

"*Paddington* won them," replied Mrs. Bird firmly. "And now he's very kindly giving them to you."

"And I've brought you a 'get well' present too, Mr. Curry," said Paddington, handing over a small white plastic object with holes in the side. "It's a special practice ball which doesn't go very far so it won't get lost."

"Thank you very much, bear," said Mr. Curry gruffly. He stared first at Paddington and then at his presents. "It's very kind of you. I was going to give you a good talking to but I shan't now."

"I should think not indeed!" exclaimed Mrs. Bird fiercely.

"Fancy you hitting a ball farther than anyone else," said Mr. Curry, still hardly able to believe his eyes or his ears.

"He didn't exactly hit it farther," said Jonathan, nudging his sister. "It only travelled farther. But Arnold Parker said it was probably a world record all the same."

"Especially for a bear," added Judy, squeezing Paddington's paw.

"A *world record*!" Mr. Curry began to look even more impressed as he listened to the others. "Very good, bear. Very good indeed!" He fingered his new clubs and then looked thoughtfully at the new practice ball. "It makes me want to have a go."

"I shouldn't if I were you," said Mrs. Brown anxiously, reading Mr. Curry's thoughts. "You don't want another accident."

"Nonsense!" exclaimed Mr. Curry, sticking his legs out of the bed. "They're letting me out soon. I feel better already." He bent down, placed the ball in the middle of the polished floor, and then, before anyone could stop him, took careful aim with one of his new clubs. "One go won't do any . . ."

Mr. Curry's voice broke off and for a second he seemed to disappear in a flurry of arms and legs. Then a loud crash shook the ward.

"Crikey!" exclaimed Jonathan. "Not again!"

"Oh, dear," said Mrs. Brown. "We did warn you . . ."

"Nurse!" bellowed Mr. Curry, as he sat up rubbing his injured leg. "Nurse! Where are you? Who left all this polish on the floor?"

The Browns exchanged glances as the doors burst open and a crowd of figures in white led by a lady in a Sister's uniform rushed into the ward.

"I think we'd better beat a hasty retreat," said Mr. Brown, voicing the thoughts of them all.

"It certainly wasn't Paddington's fault that time," said Mrs. Bird firmly.

"You know what Mr. Curry's like," said Mrs. Brown.

"Can't we tell him the rest of the story?" asked Jonathan.

Mr. Brown shook his head. "I think it'll have to wait," he said, trying to make himself heard above the hub-bub. "Anyway, I don't suppose he'll believe us."

Mrs. Brown took one last look at the crowd round Mr. Curry's bed as she led the way up the ward. "Nine miles does sound a long way for a golf ball to go," she agreed. "What a good job the rules didn't say anything about *how* it travelled."

"Fancy landing in the cab of a railway engine," said Jonathan. "No wonder the driver was waving at you."

"It was jolly good of him to have sent it back," added Judy. "What do you think, Paddington?"

Paddington considered the matter for a moment. He gave a final wave of his paw in the direction of Mr. Curry's bed and then, as the familiar voice of the Browns' neighbour rang out, he hastily followed the others through the door. "I think," he said, amid general agreement, "it's a good job I put a marmalade chunk on the side of the ball to mark it. Otherwise *no-one* would have known it was mine!"

CHAPTER THREE

A Visit to the Hospital

Mrs. Brown gave a sigh as she searched through her kitchen drawer for an elastic band. "If I see another jar of calves' foot jelly," she exclaimed with unusual vigour, "I shall scream. That's the fourth one this week. Not to mention three pots of jam, two dozen eggs and goodness knows how many bunches of grapes."

Mrs. Bird gave a snort. "If you ask me," she said grimly, "Mr. Curry will be coming out of hospital when it suits *him* and not a minute before. He knows when he's on to a good thing. Free board and lodging and everyone at his beck and call. He has a relapse every time the doctor says he's getting better."

The Browns' housekeeper took the elastic band from

Mrs. Brown and gave it a hard ping as she released it round the neck of the jar. From the expression on her face it looked as if Mr. Curry could consider himself lucky that he wasn't within range.

It was a little over a week since the Browns' neighbour had been admitted to hospital after his accident on the golf course and although X-rays and a number of probings from various doctors had revealed nothing amiss he still maintained he couldn't move his leg.

Since then the Browns had received a constant stream of postcards, notes and other messages containing urgent requests for things ranging from best grapes to newspapers, magazines, writing paper, stamps and other items too numerous to be mentioned.

At first they had been only too pleased to oblige, and with Jonathan and Judy back at school after the summer holidays Paddington in particular had spent a great deal of his time rushing round the market with his shopping basket on wheels seeing to Mr. Curry's various wants.

But after a week of visiting and listening to his complaints their enthusiasm was beginning to wear decidedly thin.

Even the hospital staff were becoming restive and the Ward Sister herself had made some very pointed remarks about the shortage of beds.

"I'm not having him here," said Mrs. Bird flatly. "That's final. And I'm certainly not having Paddington run about after him once he's home. He'll be wearing that poor bear's paws to the bone."

Paddington, who happened to arrive in the kitchen at that moment, gave a start and looked hastily at his paws, but to his relief there was no sign of anything poking through the pads and so he turned his attention to the basket of food standing on the table.

"Now you're sure you'll be all right?" asked Mrs. Brown as she carefully wedged a fruit cake into the last remaining space.

Paddington licked his lips. "I think so, Mrs. Brown," he said.

"And no picking the cherries out of the cake on the way," warned Mrs. Bird, reading his thoughts. "If Mr. Curry finds any holes we shall be getting another postcard and I've had quite enough for one week."

Paddington looked most offended at the suggestion. "Pick cherries out of Mr. Curry's cake!" he exclaimed.

Mrs. Brown broke in hastily. "Explain to him that we can't come tonight," she said. "We're all going out. There's no need to stay more than five minutes. They don't usually allow visiting in the morning but Mrs. Bird rang the Sister in charge of the ward and she said it would be all right just this once."

Paddington listened carefully to all his instructions. In his heart of hearts he wasn't too keen on visiting Mr. Curry by himself. All his visits since the accident had been with other members of the family and he had a nasty feeling that the Browns' neighbour might have one or two things to say on the subject of the golf match so he brightened at the news that he wouldn't have to stay long.

Mrs. Brown had arranged for a taxi to call and take Paddington to the hospital and a few minutes later, armed with the basket together with a small parcel of sandwiches and a thermos flask of hot cocoa in case he got delayed and missed his elevenses, he put on his duffle-coat and hat and set off.

As the taxi disappeared round the corner of Windsor Gardens Mrs. Brown and Mrs. Bird turned and went back inside the house.

"I do hope we're doing the right thing, letting him go by himself," sighed Mrs. Brown, as she closed the front door.

"I shouldn't worry about that bear," said Mrs. Bird decidedly. "He knows how to look after number one."

Mrs. Brown gave another sigh. "It wasn't Paddington I was thinking of," she replied. "It's the hospital."

Mr. Curry had been admitted to a hospital not far from Windsor Gardens. It was a busy establishment and Mrs. Brown shuddered to think of what might happen if Paddington took the wrong turning and got lost in one of its many corridors.

However, it was much too late to worry for it was only a matter of minutes before Paddington's taxi swung off the main road, passed through some large gates, and drew to a halt at the main entrance to a large brick building.

Paddington didn't often have the chance to travel in a taxi, especially by himself, and he was slightly disappointed that it was all over so quickly. Nevertheless, he felt most important as he climbed out on to the forecourt, and after thanking the driver for the ride, made his way through the entrance doors towards a desk marked RECEPTION.

"Mr. Curry?" said the uniformed man behind the desk. He ran his finger down a long list clipped to a board. "I don't recollect anyone of that name. Have you an appointment?"

"Oh, yes," said Paddington. "Mrs. Bird made one specially."

The receptionist scratched his head. "Any idea what he does?" he asked. "This is a big hospital, you know. We have all sorts of people here."

Paddington thought for a moment. "I don't think he does anything very much," he said at last. "Except grumble."

"That doesn't help a lot," said the man. "We've got one or two like that round here I can tell you. What's your name, please?"

"Brown," said Paddington promptly. "Paddington Brown. From number thirty-two Windsor Gardens."

The receptionist riffled through some more papers. "I can't find any bears down for an appointment either, let alone brown ones," he said at last. "I think I'd better pass you on to our Mr. Grant. He deals with all the difficult cases."

"Thank you very much," said Paddington gratefully. "Is he the head man?"

"That's right," said the receptionist, picking up a telephone. He was about to dial a number when he paused and looked at Paddington. "The *head* man," he repeated, his face clearing. "Bless me! Why didn't you say so before? You want the psychiatrist."

Seeing Paddington's look of surprise he leaned over his desk. "That's the chap who looks after things up here," he said, tapping his own head as he lowered his voice confidentially. "What we call the 'head-shrinker'."

Paddington began to look more and more astonished as he listened. Although he was very keen on long words he'd never heard of one as long as "psychiatrist" before, and even if his hat did feel a bit tight sometimes, particularly when he had a marmalade sandwich inside it, he wasn't at all sure that he wanted to cure it by having his head shrunk.

"I think I'd rather have my hat stretched instead," he announced with growing alarm.

It was the man's turn to look surprised as he took in Paddington's words. From where he was standing there was a very odd look about the figure on the other side of the desk, and although he couldn't find any trace of an appointment in the name of Brown, he felt sure, if the present conversation was anything to go by, that for once the rules could be by-passed.

Paddington had a very hard stare when he liked and backing away slightly the receptionist hastily consulted another list.

"There, there," he said. "There's nothing to worry about. I'll try and arrange for you to see our Mr. Heinz."

"Mr. Heinz!" exclaimed Paddington hotly. "But I wanted to see Mr. Curry. I've brought him one of Mrs. Bird's cherry cakes."

Reaching for a walking stick the man looked anxiously over his shoulder as he came round to the front of the desk. "I think you'll find Mr. Heinz much nicer," he said, eyeing Paddington warily. Realising the expression "head-shrinker" had been a bit upsetting, not to mention

49

the word "psychiatrist", he tried hard to think of another name. "He's our best 'trick-cyclist'," he added soothingly. "Just follow me."

Apart from the time when he'd spilt some hot toffee down his front by mistake and then had been unable to stand up again after it set, Paddington hadn't had a lot to do with hospitals. Even so he looked most surprised to hear that they had such things as "trick-cyclists" for the entertainment of visitors. It sounded very good value indeed and he looked around with interest as he followed the man towards a door at the far end of a long corridor.

Motioning Paddington to wait the man disappeared into the room. For a few moments there was the sound of a muffled conversation and then the door opened again.

"You're in luck's way," whispered the receptionist. "Mr. Heinz can see you straight away. He's got a free period."

Taking hold of Paddington's spare paw he propelled him through the door and then hastily closed it behind him.

After the brightness of the corridor the room seemed unusually dark. The slatted blinds were drawn over the windows and the only light came from a green shaded lamp on a desk at the far side. Apart from some cabinets and several chairs there was a long couch, rather like a padded table, in the middle of the room and behind the desk itself Paddington made out the dim figure of a man in a white coat who appeared to be examining him through a pair of unusually thick-lensed glasses.

"Come in . . . come in," said the man, turning the lamp so that it shone on Paddington's face. "Take off your coat and make yourself comfortable."

"Thank you very much," said Paddington, blinking in the strong light. He felt very pleased that he was the first one in and taking off his duffle-coat and hat he placed them on top of his basket and then settled himself down in a near-by chair.

"Have I got long to wait?" he asked, unwrapping his sandwiches.

"Oh, no," said the man in the white coat. He picked up a pen. "In fact, I'll start right away."

"I'm sorry about the cherry cake," said Paddington cheerfully.

Mr. Heinz put his pen down again. Taking off his glasses he breathed on the lenses, polished them with a handkerchief and then replaced them on his nose. "You are sorry about your *cherry cake*?" he repeated carefully.

Paddington nodded. "I'm afraid I can't let you have a slice," he said, "because Mrs. Bird doesn't want any more postcards from Mr. Curry. But you can have one of my marmalade sandwiches if you like."

Mr. Heinz gave a slight shudder as he waved aside the open bag. "Very kind of you," he said briefly, "but . . ." He paused. "Is anything the matter?" he enquired, as Paddington began peering anxiously around the room.

"It's all right, thank you, Mr. Heinz," said Paddington, turning his attention back to the man behind the desk. "I was only wondering where you keep your bike."

"My *bike?*" Mr. Heinz rose from his chair and came round to the front of the desk. "This really is a most interesting case," he exclaimed, rubbing his hands together. "The receptionist said . . . er . . ." He broke off as Paddington gave him a hard stare. "Er . . . that is . . . I may even write an article about it," he continued hastily. "I don't think I've had any bear patients before."

Helping Paddington to his feet Mr. Heinz motioned him towards the couch in the middle of the room. "I'd like you to lie on that," he said. "And then look up towards the ceiling and try to make your mind a blank."

Paddington examined the couch with interest. "Thank you very much," he exclaimed doubtfully as he clambered up, "but shall I be able to see your tricks?"

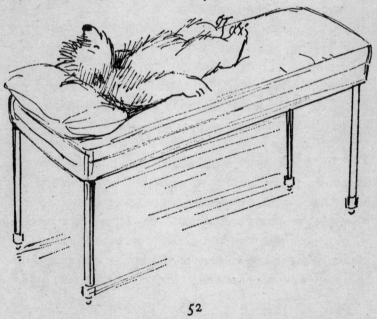

"My *tricks?*" repeated Mr. Heinz.

"The man in the hall said you were going to do some tricks," explained Paddington, beginning to look rather disappointed that nothing much was happening.

"I expect he was trying to humour ... er ... that is, keep you happy," said Mr. Heinz, making his way back to the desk.

"As a matter of fact," he continued casually, "I'd like to play a little game. It's really to test your reactions."

"A game to test my reactions?" repeated Paddington, looking more and more surprised. "I didn't know I had any."

"Oh, yes," said Mr. Heinz. "Everyone has reactions. Some people have fast ones and some have slow." He picked up his pen again. "Now I'm going to call out some words – quite quickly – and each time I call one out I want you to give me another one which has the opposite meaning ... Right?"

"Wrong," said Paddington promptly.

Mr. Heinz paused with his pen half-way to the paper. "What's the matter?" he asked crossly. "Aren't you comfortable?"

"Oh, yes," said Paddington, "but you told me to say the opposite every time you gave me a word." He sat up and gave the man behind the desk another hard stare. For someone who was supposed to be testing reactions he didn't think much of Mr. Heinz's own ones at all.

For some unknown reason Mr. Heinz appeared to be counting under his breath. "That wasn't the word, bear," he said, breathing heavily. "Wait until I give you the go-ahead. Once you start I don't want to hear anything else. I'll give you a count-down, beginning ... now. Three ... two ... one ... go!"

"Stop!" said Paddington.

Mr. Heinz opened his mouth and then appeared to change his mind. "Very good," he said grudgingly.

"Very bad," replied Paddington eagerly.

"Look here!" began Mr. Heinz, a note of panic in his voice.

"Look there!" cried Paddington wildly. Much as he had been looking forward to seeing Mr. Heinz do some tricks on his bicycle he was beginning to think the present game was much more interesting and he looked most disappointed when his last reply was greeted with silence. "Can't you think of any more words, Mr. Heinz?" he asked.

The psychiatrist spent a moment or two drumming on his desk with his fingers. He looked as if there were a number of words he would like to have said, but ignoring the temptation he picked up his pen again.

"White," he said wearily.

"Black," said Paddington, settling down again on the couch with his paws crossed and a pleased expression on his face.

"Big," said Mr. Heinz hopefully.

"Small," said Paddington promptly.

"Fast," said Mr. Heinz.

"Slow," said Paddington.

Trying several more words in quick succession Mr. Heinz began to look better pleased with the way things were going and for several minutes his pen raced across the paper as he tried to keep pace with Paddington's replies.

"Fine," he said at last, leaning back in his chair.

"Wet," exclaimed Paddington.

Mr. Heinz gave a chuckle. "We've finished . . ." he began.

"We've started," said Paddington.

"No we haven't," said Mr. Heinz crossly.

"Yes we have," cried Paddington.

"No . . . no . . . no!" shouted Mr. Heinz, thumping his desk.

"Yes . . . yes . . . yes!" cried Paddington, waving his paws in the air.

"Will you stop!" yelled Mr. Heinz.

"No I won't!" cried Paddington, nearly falling off the couch in his excitement.

Mr. Heinz looked wildly about the room. "Why did I ever take this up?" he cried, burying his face in his hands. "I should have had my head examined!"

Paddington sat up looking most surprised at the last remark. "Perhaps it needs shrinking," he said, peering at Mr. Heinz's head with interest. "I should go and see the man in the hall. He might be able to help you. He knows all about these things."

As Paddington began clambering down off the couch Mr. Heinz made a dash for the door. "I shall be gone for five minutes," he announced dramatically. "Five minutes! And if you're still here when I get back . . ."

Mr. Heinz left his sentence unfinished but from the

way he punctuated it with the slam of the door even Paddington could see that he wasn't best pleased at the way things had gone.

He peered at the closed door for several moments and then hastily gathered up his belongings. There was another door leading out of Mr. Heinz's room and after considering the matter Paddington decided to investigate this one instead of the door he'd come in by. There had been rather a nasty expression on Mr. Heinz's face when he'd left, one which he hadn't liked the look of at all, and whatever lay on the other side of the second door Paddington felt sure it couldn't be worse than the possibility of meeting the hospital's "trick-cyclist" again.

CHAPTER FOUR

Paddington Finds a Cure

Paddington closed the door behind him and stood for a moment mopping his brow. All in all he felt he'd had a narrow escape. He wasn't quite sure what he'd escaped from but he hadn't liked the look of things in the next room at all, and he was glad he'd decided to retire from the scene.

He felt even more pleased a few seconds later when the muffled sound of voices broke out on the other side of the wall. From what he could make out through the keyhole there appeared to be some kind of an argument going on and several times he distinctly heard Mr. Heinz thumping his desk. Gradually, however, the noise died away and at long last he was able to turn his attention to his new surroundings.

After the previous room it was slightly disappointing. Apart from an old hat-stand laden with white coats, the only items of furniture were a desk, on top of which was an open bag containing a number of instruments, a swivel-chair, and a big steel rack which seemed to hold a lot of large photographic negatives, and which occupied most of one wall alongside a second door.

It wasn't a bit like some of the rooms he'd seen in hospital programmes on television, with people rushing in and out pushing trolleys and barking out orders. That apart, it was also a very cold room. From his few short visits to hospitals Paddington had noticed they were very keen on fresh air and Mr. Curry's was no exception. There were three windows in the room, all much too high to reach, and all of them wide open.

Paddington began to feel pleased that Mrs. Bird had thought to provide him with the thermos flask full of hot cocoa in case he got delayed, and after several minutes had passed with no sign of anything happening he undid the top and poured some of the liquid into the cup.

A moment later Paddington let out a yell which echoed and re-echoed around the room as he danced up and down waving the cup with one paw and clutching his mouth with the other. Mrs. Bird was a great believer in making hot things as hot as possible and for once even she had excelled herself.

Hastily pouring the remains of the cocoa back into the thermos Paddington replaced the top and then began peering inside the bag on the desk in the hope of finding a mirror so that he could examine the end of his tongue.

It was while he was doing this that a thoughtful expression gradually came over his face. In the past he'd often watched programmes about hospitals on television. In fact, he was very keen on some of them, particularly the ones where there was a lot of action, and he recognised

several instruments in the bag as being identical to the ones Grant Dexter always carried when he made his rounds every Monday evening in the "Daredevil Doctor" series.

Gradually an ominous quiet descended on the room. A quiet broken only by the sound of heavy breathing and an occasional chink as Paddington investigated still deeper into the bag.

It was some while later that the door leading to the corridor slowly opened and a small figure dressed entirely in white peered out through the gap. The corridor was empty, but even if there had been anyone around, little but the closest inspection would have revealed the identity of the face behind the mask as it looked furtively first one way and then the other.

In fact, other than the unusual appearance of the coat, which reached right down to the floor, even Grant Dexter himself might have been forgiven if he'd met the wearer face to face and thought he was looking at a shortened version of his own reflection in a mirror.

Apart from the mask, the head was almost completely enveloped in a white skull-cap, and this in turn was sur-mounted by a head band and lamp. A stethoscope was draped around the neck, and although a few whiskers, which had obstinately refused to stay folded, poked out through some gaps and might have provided a clue, the rest of the face was almost entirely hidden.

Having carefully made sure no-one was coming, Paddington closed the door again and turned his attention to the photographic plates hanging on the wall.

Holding them up to the light in the way he'd seen Grant Dexter do many times before on television he peered at them hopefully, but after a few minutes he changed his mind and decided to sit down in the chair behind the desk instead. As pictures they had been most disappointing. As far as he could make out most of them showed a lot of old bones, and half of those were broken.

The swivel-chair was much more interesting and he spent some while swinging it round and round, gradually getting higher and higher until he was almost level with the top of the desk.

Waving his paws wildly in the air in the way that Mr. Heinz had done Paddington was about to give the chair a final heave when suddenly the whole world seemed to turn upside down and he found himself flying through the air. Everything went black for a moment and then he landed in a heap on the floor with what appeared to be a ton weight on top of him.

As he struggled to remove the weight Paddington heard a patter of running feet in the corridor outside and then the door suddenly burst open and a man in uniform rushed into the room.

"Where is it? Where is it?" he cried, taking aim with a large, red, fire extinguisher.

Paddington paused in his efforts to free himself. "Where is it?" he repeated in surprise.

"Blimey!" The man looked down at the figure on the floor. "Are you all right, sir?" I thought there'd been an explosion or something. One of them gas cylinders going up."

Paddington thought for a moment. "I think *I'm* all right," he said at last. "But the room's still going round."

"I'm not surprised," said the man, examining the wreckage. "Your seat's come off."

Paddington looked round. "My seat's come off!" he repeated in alarm.

"Probably ran out of thread," explained the man as he bent down to lend a helping hand. "I expect you was turning it round and round too quickly and broke the end stop . . ." He paused as he caught sight of a coloured badge in Paddington's lapel. " 'Ere," he said. "Are you one of them gentlemen from overseas?"

Paddington looked at him in amazement. "I come from Darkest Peru," he said.

"Thought so by your badge," said the man. "Oh well, we all know who you want to see, don't we?"

"Do we?" exclaimed Paddington, looking more and more surprised. "I expect Mrs. Bird rang up."

The man paused for a moment as if he hadn't heard aright. "I think you'd best come along with me," he said at last, giving Paddington a very odd look. Working in a large London hospital he'd become used to seeing strange

sights, but somehow, now that he was able to get a better view, the figure standing in front of him surpassed even his previous experience. "We don't want to keep 'is nibs waiting," he continued, hastily opening the door. " 'E don't like it much."

"I know he doesn't," agreed Paddington, looking pleased that at long last someone understood what he'd come for. "Thank you very much."

The man looked at Paddington in astonishment as he picked up his basket. " 'Ere," he said, "you're not taking *that* in with you are you?"

"I've brought it for him," explained Paddington.

"Oh, well," said the man, scratching his head. " 'Ave

it your own way. But don't say I didn't warn you. And if you want my advice you'll take them gloves off before you go in the ward."

"Take my gloves off!" exclaimed Paddington hotly as the man disappeared up the corridor. "Those aren't gloves. They're paws!"

Taking a firm grip of the basket he hurried after the man in uniform giving the back of his head some very hard stares indeed as they passed through several sets of swing-doors, along another corridor, and finally into a large, brightly lit room with a row of beds on either side.

Paddington peered down the ward. "There's Mr. Curry," he said excitedly, waving his paw in the direction of a bed at the far end. "I can see his grapes."

"I daresay it is," said his guide, putting a finger to his lips as a tall, imposing figure rose from a group gathered round a nearby bed and fixed his eyes on them. "And that's Sir Archibald. I can see 'is glares!"

"Sir Archibald?" repeated Paddington in surprise.

"That's right," said the man, looking pleased. "We're just in time. He's still doing 'is rounds."

"Look," he said, as Paddington hesitated. "You comes from overseas – right?"

"Right," said Paddington promptly.

"And you 'as a badge in yer lapel – right?"

"Right," agreed Paddington rather more doubtfully as he looked down at his coat collar.

"In that case," said the man patiently, "you must be one of Sir Archibald's students. 'E takes 'em on 'is rounds every Monday morning. And if I were you," he whispered, giving Paddington an encouraging push, "I'd go and make my apologies to 'im before I was very much older. 'E don't look best pleased to my way of thinking."

Thanking the man for his trouble Paddington picked up his basket again and hurried down the ward. He wasn't at all sure who Sir Archibald was or why he had to apologise to him, but as he drew near and caught sight of the expression on his face he had to admit that the porter was right about the great man's mood and he hastily lifted the top part of his skull-cap and let it drop back into place before he bade him good morning.

"Good afternoon's more like it," barked Sir Archibald. He glared at Paddington's outfit with a look of disgust. "It's ward rounds today — not operations. You'll be frightening the patients out of their wits.

"Now you *are* here," he continued sarcastically, pointing to the patient under examination, "perhaps you can give us the benefit of your advice. Let's have your diagnosis."

"My diagnosis!" exclaimed Paddington in alarm as he began unloading his basket. "There's a cherry cake and some calves' foot jelly, but I don't think Mrs. Bird mentioned one of those."

"Calves' foot jelly," repeated Sir Archibald, as if in a dream. "Did you say *calves' foot jelly*?"

"Grant Dexter always says it's very good if you're ill," said Paddington.

"Grant Dexter!" spluttered Sir Archibald. "And who might he be?"

66

"You don't know Grant Dexter!" exclaimed Paddington, looking most surprised. "He's in the 'Daredevil Doctor' every Monday. He's very good at curing people. All his patients get better."

"I think he'd like to know what you feel about *this* patient," hissed one of the other doctors, pointing to the man on the bed as a loud snort came from the direction of Sir Archibald.

"Have a listen on your stethoscope," murmured someone else, reaching over to undo the man's pyjama jacket. "Do *something*!"

Paddington grew more and more confused as he listened to the crumbs of advice. Picking up a headset off the bed he took the end of the stethoscope which someone else handed him and began hastily poking it on the man's chest as he listened hopefully.

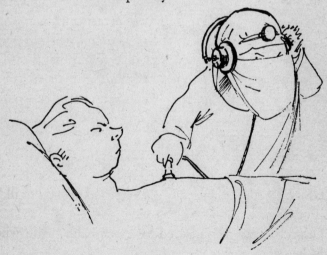

"Well," said Sir Archibald testily. "May we have your considered opinion?"

Paddington removed the headset. "I can hear someone talking," he announced, looking most surprised. "It sounds like Mrs. Dale's Diary."

"Mrs. Dale's Diary!" bellowed Sir Archibald.

"You've picked up the radio headphones by mistake," hissed someone behind Paddington. "You're supposed to use the other end of the stethoscope."

The patient sat up in bed and stared at Paddington with growing alarm. " 'Ere," he exclaimed. " 'E's not going to operate, is he? 'Cause if 'e is I'm going off 'ome right smartish."

"Rest assured, my dear sir," said Sir Archibald, "it's most unlikely." He turned and glared at Paddington. "As a doctor," he barked, "you're a disgrace to your profession. Never in all my years . . ."

"A *doctor*," exclaimed Paddington, looking even more alarmed as he pulled off his mask. "I'm not a doctor. I'm a bear. I've come to visit Mr. Curry."

Sir Archibald seemed to grow visibly larger as he drew himself up to his full height. He took in a deep breath as if about to explode, and then something in Paddington's words caused him to pause.

"Curry," he repeated. "Did you say Curry?"

"That's right," said Paddington.

"Are you a friend of his?" asked Sir Archibald suspiciously.

"Well, he lives next door," said Paddington carefully.

"But I'm not really a friend. I've brought him something to be going on with."

Sir Archibald snorted. "That's the last thing he needs," he exclaimed. "That man's entirely without scruples."

"Mr. Curry's without scruples!" repeated Paddington, looking most upset. "I thought he'd only hurt his leg."

Sir Archibald took a deep breath. "Scruples, bear," he said, "are things that stop some people taking advantage of others."

"Oh, I don't think Mr. Curry's got any of those, Sir Archibald," agreed Paddington. "Mrs. Bird's always grumbling because he takes advantage of others."

Sir Archibald and the others listened carefully as Paddington went on to explain all about the golf match and how Mr. Curry had persuaded him to act as caddie. Gradually, as the story unfolded Sir Archibald's expression changed. When it was over he gave a snort and then, as he looked first up the ward towards Mr. Curry's bed and then at Paddington, a twinkle came into his eyes.

"Are you any good at tricks, bear?" he asked thoughtfully.

"Oh, yes, Sir Archibald," said Paddington. "Bears are very good at tricks."

"Thought you might be." Sir Archibald rubbed his hands together briskly and then turned to the others. "I have a feeling this is one of those occasions when we don't stick to the book. We'll make the medicine fit the patient!"

Bending down to adjust Paddington's mask he began

whispering in his ear. It was difficult to tell what Paddington was thinking because his face was almost completely hidden again, but he nodded his head vigorously several times and then a few moments later followed the famous surgeon up the ward in the direction of Mr. Curry's bed.

Mr. Curry was reading a newspaper but when he caught sight of Sir Archibald he lowered it and gave vent to a loud groan.

"How's the patient today?" asked Sir Archibald, removing a large bowl of grapes from the bed so that he could inspect Mr. Curry's leg.

"Worse," groaned Mr. Curry. "Much worse."

"I thought you might be," said Sir Archibald cheerfully. "That's why we've decided to operate."

"Operate?" echoed Mr. Curry, suddenly growing rather pale. "Did you say operate?"

Sir Archibald nodded. "No good playing around with these things," he said. "I'd like to introduce you to . . . er . . . a colleague of mine from overseas. He specialises in legs. Does something or other to the knee. Nobody quite knows what but it seems to work very well in the jungle. Quite a few of his patients still manage to get around after a fashion."

Mr. Curry stared uneasily at the small figure hovering by the side of the bed. "It's all right," said Sir Archibald, following his glance. "There's no need to worry. We give him a box to stand on."

"I don't suppose he'll want to shake hands," he added hastily, as Mr. Curry leaned over the side of the bed.

"His own are a bit shaky."

But it was too late. A gleam of recognition came into
Mr. Curry's eyes as he caught sight of Paddington's paw.

"Bear!" he roared, recovering himself in record time.
"Bear! Up to your tricks again!"

Mr. Curry glared first at Paddington, who was looking
slightly crestfallen behind his mask now that the plan had
misfired, and then at Sir Archibald. "Tricks like this are
very bad for patients," he said slowly and loudly for the
benefit of everyone else in the ward. "I think I'm going
to have another relapse."

As Mr. Curry lay back Paddington hastily pulled off his mask and lifted the basket of food on to the bed in an effort to make amends.

"Careful, bear," growled Mr. Curry. "Mind what you're doing with that cake. I don't want any crumbs in the bed. And no taking any of the grapes when I'm not looking. If I find any empty stalks I shall know the reason why." He peered down his bed to where Paddington was busy unloading the basket. "Have you brought the . . ."

What ever else Mr. Curry had been about to say was lost for all time as suddenly, to everyone's surprise, the ward shook with a tremendous roar of pain and the sheets flew into the air as he jumped out of bed and started dancing up and down in the middle of the floor.

"Bear!" he roared, lifting his injured leg into the air like an acrobat as he tried to rub his foot. "What have you done, bear? I'll . . . I'll . . ." Mr. Curry's voice trailed away and for the second time within the space of as many seconds he left a sentence unfinished as he gazed sheepishly round at the sea of faces.

Sir Archibald turned to the Sister in charge. "It seems to me," he said, breaking the silence which followed Mr. Curry's performance, "we have another bed free in the ward after all."

"Bear's cocoa," said Sir Archibald, holding up the empty thermos. "I must remember this. Haven't seen quite such a remarkable cure in years. Must be boiling hot though!"

"I don't think I'd screwed the top of my flask on

72

properly, Mrs. Bird," explained Paddington. "It went all over Mr. Curry's foot."

Mrs. Brown and Mrs. Bird exchanged glances. So much had happened in the space of a few minutes they were feeling somewhat confused.

First their house had shaken to the sound of Mr. Curry's front door being slammed. Then a large black car had drawn up outside number thirty-two Windsor Gardens and to their amazement Paddington had emerged from the back seat, closely followed by a distinguished-looking gentleman carrying the basket of food and the thermos flask.

"All the best discoveries are made by accident," said Sir Archibald, seeing their look of puzzlement. "And in my experience some of them take quite a lot of explaining afterwards."

Sir Archibald turned to Paddington and as he did so a look of concern came over his face. "Are you all right, bear?" he asked.

Paddington felt under his coat with the end of the stethoscope he'd been given as a souvenir. "I think I'm having trouble with my beats, Sir Archibald," he announced faintly.

Sir Archibald began to look even more concerned, and then he followed Paddington's eyes as they gazed hungrily at the shopping basket.

"I think there's hope," he said gravely, turning back to the others. "Given plenty of cake and biscuits. And some hot cocoa. That's most important."

"It's funny you should say that," remarked Mrs. Bird. "I was just about to make some." She paused as Sir Archibald hovered wistfully in the doorway. "Would you care for a cup?"

"I should not only care for one," said Sir Archibald. "I should consider it a great honour. After all," he added, "inventing cures is thirsty work and bears aren't the only ones who like their elevenses."

CHAPTER FIVE

Paddington and the "Finishing Touch"

Mr. Gruber leaned on his shovel and mopped his brow with a large spotted handkerchief. "If anyone had told me three weeks ago, Mr. Brown," he said, "that one day I'd have my own patio in the Portobello Road I wouldn't have believed them."

"In fact," he continued, dusting himself down as he warmed to his subject, "if you hadn't come across that article I might *never* have had one. Now look at it!"

At the sound of Mr. Gruber's voice Paddington rose into view from behind a pile of stones. Lumps of cement clung to his fur like miniature stalactites, his hat was covered in a thin film of grey dust, and his paws – never his strongest point – looked for all the world as if they had

75

been dipped not once but many times into a mixture made up of earth, brickdust and concrete.

All the same, there was a pleased expression on his face as he put down his trowel and hurried across to join his friend near the back door of the shop so that they could inspect the result of their labours.

For in the space of a little over two weeks a great and most remarkable change had come over Mr. Gruber's back yard. A change not unlike that in the transformation scene of a Christmas pantomime.

It had all started when Paddington had come across an article in one of Mrs. Brown's old housekeeping magazines. The article in question had been about the amount of wasted space there was in a big city like London and how, with some thought and a lot of hard work, even the worst rubbish dump could be turned into a place of beauty.

The article had contained a number of photographs showing what could be done and Paddington had been so impressed by these that he'd taken the magazine along to show his friend.

Mr. Gruber kept an antique shop in the Portobello Road and although his back yard wasn't exactly a dumping ground, over the years he had certainly collected a vast amount of rubbish and in the event he'd decided to make a clean sweep of the whole area.

For several days there had been a continual stream of rag and bone men and then soon afterwards builders' lorries became a familiar sight behind the shop as they began to arrive carrying loads of broken paving-stones, sand, gravel, cement, rocks and other items of building material too numerous to be mentioned.

Taking time off each afternoon Mr. Gruber had set about the task of laying the crazy-paving whilst Paddington acted as foreman in charge of cement-mixing and filling the gaps between the stones — a job which he enjoyed no end.

At the far end of the yard Mr. Gruber erected a fence against which he planted some climbing roses and in front of this they built a rockery which was soon filled with various kinds of creeping plants.

In the middle of the patio, space had been left for a small pond containing some goldfish and a miniature fountain, whilst at the house end there now stood a carved wooden seat with room enough for two.

It was on this seat that Paddington and Mr. Gruber relaxed after their exertions each day and finished off any buns which had been left over from their morning elevenses.

"I must say we've been very lucky with the weather," said Mr. Gruber, as Paddington joined him and they took stock of the situation. "It's been a real Indian summer. Though without your help I should never have got it all done before the winter."

Paddington began to look more and more pleased as he sat down on the seat and listened to his friend, for although Mr. Gruber was a polite man, he wasn't in the habit of paying idle compliments.

Mr. Gruber gave a sigh. "If you half close your eyes and listen to the fountain, Mr. Brown," he said, "and then watch all the twinkling lights come on as it begins to get dark, you might be anywhere in the world."

"There's only one thing missing," he continued, after a moment's pause.

Paddington, who'd almost nodded off in order to enjoy a dream in which it was a hot summer's night and he and Mr. Gruber were sipping cocoa under the stars, sat up in surprise.

"What's that, Mr. Gruber?" he asked anxiously, in case he'd left out something important by mistake.

"I don't know," said Mr. Gruber dreamily. "But there's something missing. What the whole thing needs is some kind of finishing touch. A statue or a piece of stonework. I can't think what it can be."

Mr. Gruber gave a shiver as he rose from his seat, for once the sun disappeared over the rooftops a chill came into the air. "We shall just have to put our thinking caps on, Mr. Brown," he said, "and not take them off again until we come up with something. It's a pity to spoil the ship for a ha'p'orth of tar."

" 'Adrian Crisp – Garden Ornaments'," exclaimed Mrs. Bird. "What's that bear up to now?" She held up a small piece of paper. "I found this under his bed this morning. It looks as if it's been cut from a magazine. *And* my best carrier bag is missing!"

Mrs. Brown glanced up from her sewing. "I expect it's

got something to do with Mr. Gruber's patio," she
replied. "Paddington *was* rather quiet when he came in
last night. He said he had his thinking cap on and I
noticed him poking about looking for my scissors."

Mrs. Bird gave a snort. "That bear's bad enough when
he *doesn't* think of things," she said grimly. "There's no
knowing what's likely to happen when he really puts his
mind to it. Where is he, anyway?"

"I think he went out," said Mrs. Brown vaguely. She
took a look at the scrap of paper Mrs. Bird had brought
downstairs. " 'Works of art in stone bought and sold. No
item too small or too large'."

"I don't like the sound of that last bit," broke in Mrs.
Bird. "I can see Mr. Gruber ending up with a statue of
the Duke of Wellington in his back garden."

"I hope not," said Mrs. Brown. "I can't picture even
Paddington trying to get a statue on to a London bus. At
least," she added uneasily, "I don't think I can."

Unaware of the detective work going on at number thirty-two Windsor Gardens, Paddington peered around with a confused look on his face. Altogether he was in a bit of a daze. In fact he had to admit that he'd never ever seen anything quite like Mr. Crisp's establishment before.

It occupied a large wilderness of a garden behind a ramshackle old house some distance away from the Browns', and as far as the eye could see every available square inch of ground was covered by statues, seats, pillars, balustrades, posts, stone animals – the list was endless. Even Adrian Crisp himself, as he followed Paddington in and out of the maze of pathways, seemed to have only a very vague idea of what was actually there.

"Pray take your time, my dear chap," he exclaimed, dabbing his face with a silk handkerchief as they reached

their starting point for the third time. "Some of these items are hundreds of years old and I think they'll last a while yet. There's no hurry at all."

Paddington thanked Mr. Crisp and then peered thoughtfully at a pair of small stone lions standing near by. They were among the first things

80

he'd seen on entering the garden and all in all they seemed to fit most closely what he had in mind.

"I think I like the look of those, Mr. Crisp," he exclaimed, bending down in order to undo the secret compartment in his suitcase.

Adrian Crisp followed the direction of Paddington's gaze and then lifted a label attached to one of the lion's ears. "Er . . . I'm not sure if you'll be able to manage it," he said doubtfully. "The pair are one hundred and seventy pounds."

Paddington remained silent for a moment as he tried to picture the combined weight of one hundred and seventy jars of marmalade. "I quite often bring all Mrs. Bird's shopping home from the market," he said at last.

Adrian Crisp allowed himself a laugh. "Oh, dear me," he said. "I'm afraid we're talking at cross-purposes. That isn't the weight. That's how much they cost."

"One hundred and seventy pounds!" exclaimed Paddington, nearly falling over backwards with surprise.

Mr. Crisp adjusted his bow tie and gave a slight cough as he caught sight of the expression on Paddington's face. "I might be able to let you have a small faun for fifty pounds," he said reluctantly. "I'm afraid the tail's fallen off but it's quite a bargain. If I were to tell you where it came from originally you'd have quite a surprise."

Paddington, who looked as if nothing would surprise him ever again, sat down on his suitcase and stared mournfully at Mr. Crisp.

"I can see you won't be tempted, my dear fellow,"

said Mr. Crisp, trying to strike a more cheerful note. "Er . . . how much did you actually think of paying?"

"I was *thinking* of sixpence," said Paddington hopefully.

"*Sixpence!*" If Paddington had been taken by surprise a moment before Adrian Crisp looked positively devastated.

"I could go up to four shillings if I break into my bun money, Mr. Crisp," said Paddington hastily.

"Don't strain your resources too much, bear," said Mr. Crisp, delicately removing a lump of leaf mould from his suede shoes. "This isn't a charitable institution, you know," he continued, eyeing Paddington with disfavour. "It's been a lifetime's work collecting these items and I can't let them go for a song."

"I'm afraid I've only got four shillings," said Paddington firmly.

Adrian Crisp took a deep breath. "I suppose I might be able to find you one or two bricks," he said sarcastically. "You'll have to arrange your own transport, of course, but . . ." He broke off as he caught Paddington's eye. Paddington had a very hard stare when he liked and his present one was certainly one of the most powerful he'd ever managed.

"Er . . ." Mr. Crisp glanced round unhappily and then his face suddenly lit up as he caught sight of something just behind Paddington. "The very thing!" he exclaimed. "I could certainly let you have *that* for four shillings."

Paddington turned and looked over his shoulder.

"Thank you very much, Mr. Crisp," he said doubtfully. "What is it?"

"*What is it?*" Mr. Crisp looked slightly embarrassed. I think it fell off something a long time ago," he said hastily. "I'm not sure what. Anyway, my dear fellow, for four shillings you don't ask what it is. You should be thankful for small mercies."

Paddington didn't like to say anything but from where he was standing Mr. Crisp's object seemed rather a large mercy. It was big and round and it looked for all the world like a giant stone football. However, he carefully counted out his four shillings and handed the money over before the owner had time to change his mind.

"Thank you, I'm sure," said Mr. Crisp, reluctantly taking possession of a sticky collection of coins made up of several threepenny bits, a number of pennies, and a large pile of ha'pennies. He paused as Paddington turned his attention to the piece of stone. "I shouldn't do that if I were you," he began.

But it was too late. Almost before the words were out of his mouth there came the sound of tearing paper. Paddington stood looking at the two string handles in his paw and then at the sodden remains of brown paper underneath the stone. "That was one of Mrs. Bird's best carrier bags," he exclaimed hotly.

"I did try to warn you, bear," said Mr. Crisp. "You've got a bargain there. That stone's worth five shillings of anybody's money just for the weight alone. If you like to hang on a moment I'll roll it outside for you."

Paddington gave Mr. Crisp a hard stare. "You'll roll it outside for me," he repeated, hardly able to believe his ears. "But I've got to get it all the way back to the Portobello Road."

Mr. Crisp took a deep breath. "I might be able to find you a cardboard box," he said sarcastically, "but I'm afraid we expect you to bring your own string for anything under five shillings."

Mr. Crisp looked as if he'd had enough dealings with bear customers for one day and when, a few minutes later, he ushered Paddington out through the gates he bade him a hasty farewell and slammed the bolts shut on the other side with an air of finality.

Taking a deep breath Paddington placed his suitcase carefully on top of the box, and then clasping the whole lot firmly with both paws, he began staggering up the road in the general direction of Windsor Gardens and the Portobello Road.

If the stone object had seemed large amongst all the

other odds and ends in Mr. Crisp's garden, now that he actually had it outside it seemed enormous. Several times he had to stop in order to rest his paws and once, when he accidentally stepped on a grating outside a row of shops, he nearly overbalanced and fell through a window.

Altogether he was thankful when at long last he peered round the side of his load and caught sight of a small queue standing beside a familiar looking London Transport sign not far ahead.

He was only just in time for as he reached the end of the queue a bus swept to a halt beside the stop and a voice from somewhere upstairs bade everyone to "hurry along."

"Quick," said a man, coming to his rescue, "there's an empty seat up the front."

Before Paddington knew what was happening he found himself being bundled on to the bus whilst several other willing hands in the crowd took charge of the cardboard box for him and placed it in the gangway behind the driver's compartment.

He barely had time to raise his hat in order to thank everyone for their trouble before there was a sudden jerk and the bus set off again on its journey.

Paddington fell back into the seat mopping his brow and as he did so he looked out of the window in some surprise. Although, as far as he could remember, it was a fine day outside, he'd distinctly heard what sounded like the ominous rumble of thunder.

It had seemed quite close for a second or two and he peered anxiously up at the sky in case there was any lightning about, but as far as he could make out there wasn't a cloud anywhere in sight.

At that moment there came a clattering of heavy feet on the stairs as the conductor descended to the bottom deck.

" 'Ullo, 'ullo," said a disbelieving voice a second later. "What's all this 'ere?"

Paddington glanced round to see what was going on and as he did so his eyes nearly fell out of their sockets.

The cardboard box, which a moment before had stood neatly and innocently beside him, now had a gaping hole in its side. Worse still, the cause of the hole was now resting at the other end of the gangway!

"Is this yours?" asked the conductor, pointing an accusing finger first at the stone by his feet and then at Paddington.

"I think it must be," said Paddington vaguely.

"Well, I'm not 'aving no bear's boulders on my bus," said the conductor. He indicated a notice just above his head. "It says 'ere plain enough — 'parcels may be left under the staircase by permission of the conductor' — and I ain't given me permission. Nor likely to neither. Landed on me best corn it did."

"It isn't a bear's boulder," exclaimed Paddington hotly. "It's Mr. Gruber's 'finishing touch'."

The conductor reached up and rang the bell. "It'll be your finishing touch and all if I have any more nonsense," he said crossly. "Come on — off with you."

The conductor looked as if he'd been about to say a

great deal more on the subject of bear passengers in general and Paddington and his piece of stonework in particular when he suddenly broke off. For as the bus ground to a halt the stone suddenly began trundling back up the gangway, ending its journey with a loud bang against the wall at the driver's end.

A rather cross-looking face appeared for a moment at the window just above it. Then the bus surged forward again and before anyone had time to stop it the stone began rolling back down the gangway, landing once more at the conductor's feet.

"I've 'ad just about enough of this!" he exclaimed, hopping up and down as he reached for the bell. "We've gone past two requests and a compulsory as it is."

The words were hardly out of his mouth when a by now familiar thundering noise followed by an equally familiar thump drowned the excited conversation from the other passengers in the bus.

For a moment or two the bus seemed to hover shaking in mid-air as if one half wanted to go on and the other half wanted to stay. Then, with a screech of brakes, it pulled in to the side of the road and as it ground to a halt the driver jumped out and came hurrying round to the back.

"Why don't you make up your mind?" he cried, addressing his mate on the platform. "First you rings the bell to say you want to stop. Then you bangs on me panel to say go on. Then you rings the bell again. Then it's bang on me panel. I don't know whether I'm on me head or me heels, let alone driving a bus."

"I like that!" exclaimed the conductor. "*I* banged on your panel. It was that blessed bear with 'is boulder what done it."

"A bear with a boulder?" repeated the driver disbelievingly. "Where? I can't see him."

The conductor looked up the gangway and then his face turned white. "He *was* there," he said. "And he had this boulder what kept rolling up and down the gangway."

"There he is!" he exclaimed triumphantly. "I told you so!"

He pointed down the road to where in the distance a small brown figure could be seen hurrying after a round, grey object as it zigzagged down the road. "It must have fallen off the last time you stopped."

"Well, I hope he catches it before it gets to the Portobello Road," said the driver. "If it gets in amongst all them barrows there's no knowing what'll happen."

"Bears!" exclaimed the conductor bitterly, as a sudden thought struck him. "He didn't even pay for 'is fare let alone extra for 'is boulder."

Paddington and Mr. Gruber settled themselves comfortably on the patio seat. After all his exertions in the early part of the day Paddington was glad of a rest and the sight of a tray laden with two mugs, a jug of cocoa and a plate of buns into the bargain was doubly welcome.

Mr. Gruber had been quite overwhelmed when Paddington presented him with the piece of stone.

"I don't know when I've had such a nice present, Mr. Brown," he said. "Or such an unexpected one. How you managed to get it all the way here by yourself I really don't know."

"It was rather heavy, Mr. Gruber," admitted Paddington. "I nearly strained my resources."

"Fancy that conductor calling it a boulder," continued Mr. Gruber, looking at the stone with a thoughtful expression on his face.

"Even Mr. Crisp didn't seem to know quite what it was," said Paddington. "But he said it was a very good bargain."

"I'm sure he was right," agreed Mr. Gruber. He examined the top of the stone carefully and ran his fingers over the top, which appeared to have a flatter surface than the rest and was surrounded by a rim, not unlike a small tray. "Do you know what I think it is, Mr. Brown?"

Paddington shook his head.

"I think it's an old Roman cocoa stand," said Mr. Gruber.

"A Roman cocoa stand," repeated Paddington excitedly.

"Well, perhaps it isn't exactly Roman," replied Mr. Gruber truthfully. "But it's certainly very old and I can't think of a better use for it."

He reached over for the jug, filled both mugs to the brim with steaming liquid and then carefully placed them on top of the stone. To Paddington's surprise they fitted exactly.

"There," said Mr. Gruber with obvious pleasure. "I don't think anyone could find a better finishing touch for their patio than that, Mr. Brown. Not if they tried for a thousand years."

CHAPTER SIX

Everything Comes to Those Who Wait

Mrs. Bird gave a groan as the sound of several voices raised in song followed almost immediately by a sharp rat-tat-tat on the front door echoed down the hall.

"Not again," she said, putting down her sewing. "That's the fifth lot of carol singers in half an hour. I shall be glad when Christmas is here."

"I'll go," said Mr. Brown grimly.

"I should be careful what you say, Henry," warned Mrs. Brown. "Don't forget Paddington's out doing the same thing."

Mr. Brown paused at the lounge door. "What!" he exclaimed. "Paddington's out *carol singing*? You don't mean to say you let him go!"

"He seemed very keen on the idea," replied Mrs. Brown. "Jonathan and Judy are with him so he should be all right."

"I think they're collecting for some kind of party," broke in Mrs. Bird, coming to her rescue. "It's all rather secret."

"Well, I hope whoever they are they're not relying on Paddington's efforts for their Christmas entertainment," said Mr. Brown, feeling in his pocket. "Otherwise they're in for a pretty bleak time. Have you ever heard him sing?"

"He went out by himself the other evening before Jonathan and Judy broke up for their holidays," said Mrs. Brown. "And he did quite well considering."

"Two bananas, a button and some French francs," replied Mr. Brown. "And the bananas looked as if they'd seen better days."

"I wouldn't say singing was exactly his strong point," agreed Mrs. Brown reluctantly, "but he's been practising quite hard up in his bedroom just lately."

"There's no need to tell me *that*," remarked Mr. Brown feelingly. "He had me out of bed twice last night. I thought it was the blessed cats!" He turned to go as once again the familiar strains of *Good King Wenceslaus* filled the air, and then his face brightened as a sudden thought struck him. "I suppose," he said, "it is *one* way of getting our own back!"

Had they been able to overhear the last remark not only Paddington, but both Jonathan and Judy would have

been most upset, but fortunately for the sake of peace in
the Browns' household they were much too far away at
that moment, and in any case they had other more
important problems to occupy their minds.

In particular there was the matter of the amount they
had been able to collect from their evening's work.

"One and fourpence ha'penny," said Jonathan bitterly,
as he shone his torch into the cardboard box which they'd

been using for the takings. "A measly one and fourpence ha'penny."

"It's not too bad," said Judy, "considering only six people have answered the door."

"They can't have *all* been out," said Jonathan. "I wish we'd started our school holidays earlier. The trouble is everyone's getting fed up by now. I reckon we've left it a bit late."

"Perhaps we could say we're collecting for *next* Christmas," said Paddington hopefully.

It had been Paddington's idea to collect some money for the annual children's party at the hospital and he was beginning to feel a bit guilty about the whole affair, especially as they'd set themselves a target of ten pounds.

Judy squeezed his paw. "I don't think they'd be very pleased if we said that," she confided. "Never mind. We'll think of something. We mustn't give up now."

"Suppose we all separate," said Jonathan thoughtfully. "If we do that we ought to collect three times as much."

"We needn't go far away," he added, reading Judy's thoughts. "In fact, we needn't really lose sight of each other. Paddington can have the torch – then he can signal if he wants anything."

"All right," said Judy reluctantly. She glanced at the surrounding houses. "I'll take that one on the corner."

"Bags I have a go at the one over there with the Christmas tree in the window," exclaimed Jonathan. "Which one are you going to do, Paddington?"

Paddington considered the matter for a moment as he

peered round at all the houses. "I think I'd like to try that one over there," he announced, pointing towards an imposing looking house standing slightly apart from the rest, and from which there came the distinct sounds of a party in full swing.

"Come on, then," exclaimed Jonathan impatiently. "We shan't get anywhere if we don't make a start. We'll meet back here in half an hour."

"Don't forget," called Judy. "If you get into any trouble signal with the torch."

"Send an S.O.S.," shouted Jonathan. "Three short flashes, then three long ones and three short ones to follow."

After testing his torch carefully in order to make sure it was working, Paddington hurried up the path towards the front door of the house he'd chosen, cleared his throat several times, and then knocked loudly on the front door. He wasn't the sort of bear who believed in taking too many chances and with so much noise going on inside the house he didn't want to knock *after* he'd sung his carol and then find no one had heard him.

He opened his mouth and was about to launch forth into *Hark the Herald Angels Sing* when to his surprise the door suddenly opened and a lady stood framed in the light from the hall.

"Thank goodness you've come," she exclaimed. "I was beginning to get quite worried."

"I'm Mrs. Smith-Cholmley," she added, as she opened the door wider and motioned Paddington to enter.

Paddington raised his hat politely as he stepped into the hall. "Thank you very much," he exclaimed. "I'm Paddington Brown."

For some reason the welcoming expression on Mrs. Smith-Cholmley's face began to fade. "Have you done much waiting?" she asked.

"Oh, no," said Paddington, looking round with interest. "I've only just got here."

"I mean have you had any previous experience of waiting?" said Mrs. Smith-Cholmley impatiently.

Paddington considered the matter for a moment. "I had to wait for a bus the other day when Mrs. Bird took me out shopping," he said thoughtfully.

Mrs. Smith-Cholmley gave a rather high-pitched laugh. "Mr. Bridges at the agency said waiters were a bit short this year," she remarked, looking down at Paddington, "but I didn't think he meant . . . I mean . . . I thought he meant they were a job to get . . . that is . . ." her voice trailed away.

"Oh, well, at least they've sent *someone*," she continued brightly, avoiding Paddington's gaze. "We're having a little dinner-party and it's long past time to serve the first course. You'd better go straight to the kitchen and see Vladimir. He's beside himself."

"Vladimir's beside himself!" exclaimed Paddington, looking most surprised.

"He's the chef," explained Mrs. Smith-Cholmley. "And if he doesn't get some help soon I'm sure he'll do something nasty with his chopper. He was looking very gloomy the last time I saw him." She glanced down at Paddington's paw. "Let me take your torch. I'm sure you won't want that."

"I think I'll keep it if you don't mind," said Paddington firmly. "I may want to send some signals."

"Just as you wish," said Mrs. Smith-Cholmley, giving him a strange look. She led the way down a long corridor and then paused before a door at the end as she opened her handbag. "Here's your five pounds."

"My five pounds!" Paddington's eyes nearly popped out of his head as he stared at the crisp new note in his paw.

"That's what I usually pay," said Mrs. Smith-Cholmley. "But I'd like you to start straight away."

"Thank you very much," said Paddington, still hardly able to believe his good fortune. Five pounds seemed a great deal of money to pay for a carol even if it was nearly Christmas and he hastily put the note into the secret compartment of his suitcase in case Mrs. Smith-Cholmley changed her mind when she discovered he only knew one verse.

As Paddington stood up, opened his mouth, and the first few notes of *Hark the Herald Angels Sing* rang through the hall the colour seemed to drain from Mrs. Smith-Cholmley's face. "That's all I need," she cried, putting her hands to her ears. "A singing waiter!"

Paddington broke off in the middle of his opening chorus. "A singing waiter!" he repeated, looking most upset. "I'm not a singer — I'm a bear."

Mrs. Smith-Cholmley gave a shudder. "I can tell that," she said, opening the kitchen door. "And I shall certainly have something to say to Mr. Bridges about it in the morning. In the meantime you'd better start earning your money. Everyone's absolutely ravenous."

Without waiting for a reply she pushed Paddington through the door and hastily closed it behind him.

"Hah!"

Paddington jumped as a figure in white overalls and a tall white hat rose from behind a pile of saucepans and advanced towards him. "So! You have come at last. Quick . . . off viz your duffle-coat and out viz your arms."

Paddington stood blinking in the strong white light of the kitchen, hardly able to believe his eyes let alone his ears. In fact he was so taken aback at the sudden strange turn of events that before he knew what was happening he found his duffle-coat had been removed and he was standing with his arms outstretched while the man in white overalls balanced a row of bowls on each of them.

"Quick! Quick!" shouted Vladimir, snapping his fingers. "Get cracking viz your mulligatawnies."

"Get cracking with my mulligatawnies!" repeated Paddington carefully, finding his voice at last but hardly daring to breathe in case any of the bowls overbalanced.

"Zee soup," said Vladimir impatiently. "It is getting cold and on such short arms it is difficult to balance so much."

Paddington blinked several times to make sure he wasn't dreaming and then closed his eyes in order to count up to ten but before he had time to reach even two he found himself being bundled back out of the kitchen and when he opened them again he was standing outside yet another door behind which could be heard the chatter of voices.

"Quick," hissed Vladimir, giving Paddington a firm push. "In here."

A buzz of excitement broke out in the room as Paddington entered, and several of the guests applauded.

"What a delightful idea, Mabel," said one lady. "Having a bear for a waiter. Trust you to think up something unusual."

Mrs. Smith-Cholmley gave a sickly smile. "Oh, it wasn't really my idea," she said truthfully. "It's just happened. But it makes a nice change."

She eyed Paddington warily as he arrived at the table with his load of bowls, but to her relief, apart from the fact that he was breathing rather heavily down the neck of one of her guests who happened to be in the way, there was little she could find fault with.

"I think we'd better give you a hand," she said hastily, when nothing happened. "We don't want any nasty accidents."

"Thank you very much," said Paddington gratefully as one by one the various diners relieved him of his burden. "It's a bit difficult with paws."

"Talking of paws," said the man Paddington had been

standing behind, "you've got one of yours in my soup."

"Oh, that's all right," said Paddington politely. "It isn't very hot."

The man eyed the bowl distastefully. "May I give you a tip?" he asked.

"Oh, yes please," said Paddington eagerly. Now that he was getting used to the idea of being a waiter he was beginning to enjoy himself and after giving his paw a hasty lick in order to remove some soup which had accidently overflowed he held it out hopefully.

"Don't carry quite so much next time," said the man sternly, as he helped himself to a roll, "then it won't happen."

Mrs. Smith-Cholmley gave a nervous giggle as she caught sight of the expression on Paddington's face. "I think I should see how Vladimir's getting on with the next course," she called out hastily.

Paddington gave the man with the roll one final, long hard stare and then, after collecting several empty soup dishes, he made his way towards the door. The carol singing, not to mention the waiting, had made him feel more than usually hungry and Mrs. Smith-Cholmley's words reminded him of the fact that during his brief spell in the kitchen he'd noticed some very interesting smells coming from beneath the lids of Vladimir's saucepans.

Although he still wasn't entirely sure what was happening Paddington didn't want to run the risk of it all coming to an end before he'd had time to investigate the matter. What with one thing and another serving the first course had taken rather longer than he'd expected and he hurried back down the corridor as fast as his legs would carry him.

To his surprise, when he got back to the kitchen Vladimir was no longer dressed in white. His chef's hat was lying in a crumpled ball in the middle of the floor and Vladimir himself was standing by the back door clad in a black overcoat and muffler.

"I may go back to Poland," he announced gloomily when he caught sight of Paddington.

"Oh, dear," said Paddington. "I hope nothing's wrong."

"*Everything* is wrong," said Vladimir. He thumped his chest. "I Vladimir, I who have cooked for ze crowned 'eads of Europe. I, who have 'ad princes wait while I add ze final touches to my creations. I, Vladimir, am reduced to zis. Waiting . . . all ze time I am kept waiting." He waved his hand disconsolately in the air. "My soup, she is cold. My entrecots, zey are cold . . ."

"Your entrecots are cold!" repeated Paddington, looking most upset.

Vladimir nodded. "My beautiful steak – ruined!" He pointed towards a grill laden with slowly congealing pieces of meat which stood on a near-by table.

"I 'ad to take them from the stove or they would 'ave been burned to a cinder." He reached out and clasped Paddington's paw. "They are yours, my friend. In the saucepans you will find the vegetables. You may serve it as you think fit. I, Vladimir, no longer care. Good-bye, my friend . . . and good luck!"

Worn out by his long speech Vladimir paused by the back door, waved his hand dramatically in the air, and then disappeared from view, leaving Paddington rooted to the spot in astonishment.

But if Paddington was upset by the sight of Vladimir's sudden departure, Mrs. Smith-Cholmley looked even more upset when, some while later, she caught sight of her steak.

By the time he'd got around to serving all the various vegetables and carried all the plates into the dining-room things had gone from bad to worse. Even putting some of the pieces of steak in an electric toaster hadn't helped matters, particularly as several of them had popped out and fallen on the floor before he'd had a chance to catch them.

Looking at his offering Paddington had to admit that he didn't really fancy it much himself and he felt pleased he'd taken time off to have his own snack before serving the others.

"If there's anything wrong with the Baked Alaska," hissed Mrs. Smith-Cholmley, endeavouring to glare at Paddington with one half of her face and smile at her guests with the other, "I shall insist on Vladimir giving me my money back."

"Baked Alaska," she repeated through her teeth as she saw the look of surprise on Paddington's face. "It's a special surprise for my guests and I want it to be absolutely perfect."

If Paddington's spirits sank as he made his way slowly

back down the corridor towards the kitchen they fell still more during the next few minutes as he peered hopefully at first one cookery book and then another.

Although Mrs. Smith-Cholmley had only spoken of asking the chef for his money back he had a nasty feeling that when it came down to it and she found Vladimir had disappeared his own five pounds might not be too safe.

Mrs. Smith-Cholmley had a large collection of cookery books from many different parts of the world, but not one of them so much as mentioned the dish he was looking for.

It was as he closed the last of the books that Paddington caught sight of a near-by low hanging shelf which he hadn't noticed before and as he did so he gave a sudden start. For there, right in front of his eyes, was a row of tins one of which was labelled with the very words he'd been looking for.

Hardly daring to close his eyes in case the tin disappeared Paddington spent the next few minutes hastily making his preparations. First he turned the knob over the oven to read "high", then he looked around for a suitable dish. After carefully checking the thermometer in order to make sure the oven was hot enough he emptied the contents of the tin into the dish and placed it inside the cooker.

Normally the only thing Paddington had against cooking was the amount of time it took for anything to happen, but on this occasion he hadn't long to wait. In fact, he'd hardly had time to settle down on his suitcase and make himself comfortable before several whiffs of black smoke rose from the cooker and the pleased expression on his face was rapidly replaced by a look of alarm as a most unappetising smell began to fill the kitchen.

Hurrying across the room he tore open the oven door only to stagger back as a cloud of thick, black smoke poured out.

Holding his nose with one paw he picked up his torch with the other and peered mournfully at the contents of the baking-dish as it sizzled and bubbled inside the oven.

Paddington was a hopeful bear at heart, but although Mrs. Smith-Cholmley had definitely said she wanted to

surprise her guests, he couldn't help feeling as he trund-
led a trolley laden with portions of his sweet down the
corridor some while later that his efforts might prove
rather more than she'd bargained for.

Giving vent to a deep sigh he took a firm grip of his
torch as he tapped on the dining-room door. Jonathan had
told him to send out a distress signal if he was in trouble
and he had a nasty idea in the back of his mind that the
moment to take his advice was not too far away.

Mr. Brown stared at Paddington as if he could hardly
believe his eyes. "Do you mean to say," he exclaimed,
"that you actually served this Mrs. Smith-Cholmley
baked *elastic?*"

Paddington nodded unhappily. "I found some rubber
bands in a tin, Mr. Brown," he explained.

"He didn't realise Mrs. Smith-Cholmley said 'Baked
Alaska'," said Judy. "That's a sort of ice-cream dish
cooked in the oven."

"It was just after that he sent out his S.O.S.," added
Jonathan.

"I'm not surprised," exclaimed Mrs. Bird. "It's a
wonder some of the guests didn't send one as well."

"They were jolly nice about it all," said Judy. "When
the real waiter turned up and they discovered Paddington
had really only come to sing a carol they made us all stay."

"He'd met Vladimir on the way too," added Jonathan.

"*Vladimir?*" echoed Mr. Brown. He was rapidly losing track of the conversation. "Who's Vladimir?"

"The chef," explained Judy. "When he discovered the mistake he came back after all and he made some real baked Alaska so everyone was happy."

"We sang some carols afterwards," said Jonathan. "And we collected over three pounds. That means we've nearly reached our target."

Judy gave a sigh. "The Baked Alaska was super," she said dreamily. "I could eat some more."

"So could I," agreed Jonathan.

Paddington licked his lips. "I expect I could make you some if you like, Mr. Brown," he exclaimed.

"Not in *my* kitchen," said Mrs. Bird sternly. "I'm not having any young bear's elastic baked in my oven!"

She paused at the door. "Mind you," she added casually, "as it happens we were having some ice-cream for supper . . ."

"I must say it sounds rather nice," said Mrs. Brown.

Mr. Brown stroked his moustache thoughtfully, "I could toy with some myself," he agreed. "How about you, Paddington?"

Paddington considered the matter for a moment. If one thing stood out above all others in his mind from the evening's adventure it was the memory of Vladimir's Baked Alaska and he felt sure that an Alaska baked by Mrs. Bird would be nicer still.

The Browns' housekeeper looked unusually pink about the ears as she raised her hands at the noisy approval which greeted Paddington as he gave voice to his thoughts.

"Compliments are always nice," she said. "Especially genuine ones."

"But if you ask me," she continued, pausing at the door, "bear's compliments are the nicest ones of all and they certainly deserve the biggest helpings!"

CHAPTER SEVEN

Paddington Goes to Town

Mr. Brown lowered his evening paper and looked around the room at the rest of the family. "Do you realise something?" he said. "It's nearly Christmas and we haven't been up to Town to see the decorations yet!"

Paddington pricked up his ears at Mr. Brown's words. "I don't think I've *ever* been to see them, Mr. Brown," he said. "Not the Christmas ones."

The Browns stopped what they were doing and stared at him in wide-eyed amazement. Paddington had been with them for so long, and was so much a part of their lives, they'd somehow taken it for granted that he'd seen the Christmas decorations at some time or another and it didn't seem possible for such an important matter to have been overlooked.

"Mercy me, I do believe that bear's right," said Mrs. Bird. "We've seen the ordinary lights several times, and we've seen the decorations during daylight when we've been doing our Christmas shopping, but we've never been up specially. Not at night."

"Gosh, Dad," exclaimed Jonathan. "Can we go to-night? It's years since we went."

Mr. Brown looked first at his watch and then at his wife and Mrs. Bird. "I'm game," he said. "How about you?"

Mrs. Brown looked at Mrs. Bird. "I've done everything I want to do," said their housekeeper. "I'm very well advanced this year. I only have to take my mince pies out of the oven and I shall be ready."

"May we go, Daddy?" implored Judy. "*Please?*"

Mr. Brown glanced round the room with a twinkle in his eye. "What do you say, Paddington?" he asked. "Would you like to?"

"*Yes, please,* Mr. Brown," exclaimed Paddington eagerly. "I should like that very much indeed."

Paddington was always keen on trips, especially unexpected ones with the whole family, and when Mr. Brown announced that he would call in on the way and pick up Mr. Gruber into the bargain he grew more and more excited.

For the next half an hour there was great pandemonium in number thirty-two Windsor Gardens as everyone rushed around getting ready for the big event and even Paddington himself went so far as to rub a flannel over his whiskers while Judy gave his fur a brush down.

It was a very gay party of Browns that eventually set off in Mr. Brown's car and shortly afterwards the hilarity was increased still further as Mr. Gruber emerged from his shop carrying a camera and some flashbulbs, several of which he used in order to take photographs of the assembly.

"You're not the only one who hasn't been to see the Christmas decorations, Mr. Brown," he said, addressing Paddington as he squeezed into the back seat alongside Mrs. Bird, Jonathan and Judy. "I've never been either and I want to make the most of it."

If the Browns had been surprised to discover that Paddington had never seen the lights they were even more astonished at this latest piece of information and Paddington himself was so taken aback he quite forgot to give his usual paw signal as they swung out of the Portobello Road.

Mr. Gruber chuckled at the effect of his words. "People never do see things that are on their own doorstep," he said wisely. "I must say it'll be a great treat. I've heard they're particularly good this year."

As they drove along Mr. Gruber went on to explain to Paddington how each year all the big shops in London got together in order to festoon the streets with huge decorations made up of hundreds of coloured lights, and also how each year an enormous Christmas tree was sent from Norway as a gift to the people of London, and how it was always placed in a position of honour in Trafalgar Square.

It all sounded most interesting and the excitement mounted as they drew nearer and nearer to the centre of London.

Mr. Gruber coughed as Paddington jumped up in his seat and began waving his paws in the direction of a cluster of green lights some distance ahead.

"I have a feeling those are traffic lights, Mr. Brown," he said tactfully, as they changed to amber. "But just you wait until you see the real thing."

At that moment the lights suddenly changed again, this time to red, and the car screeched to a halt. "I'm not surprised he mistook them," grumbled Mr. Brown. "It's a wonder he could see anything at all. If we're not careful we shall have a nasty accident." Rather pointedly he picked up a duster and began wiping the glass in front of him. "Bear's steam all over my windscreen! People will begin to think we're boiling a kettle in here or something."

"It's always worse when he's excited, Henry," said Mrs. Brown, coming to Paddington's rescue as he sank back into his seat looking most offended.

"If I were you," she continued, "I'd stop somewhere. We shall see much more if we walk."

Mrs. Brown's suggestion met with whole-hearted approval from the rest of the family. They were beginning to feel a bit cramped, and some while later, having disentangled the car from the maze of traffic and found somewhere to park, even Mr. Brown had to agree that it was a good idea as they climbed out and set off on foot down one of the busy London thoroughfares.

It was a crisp, clear night and the pavement on either side of the street was thronged with people gazing into shop windows, staring up at the decorations which seemed to hang overhead like a million golden stars in the sky, or simply, like the Browns, strolling leisurely along drinking it all in.

Near by, on the Browns' side of the street, a long queue of people were waiting to go into a cinema, and somewhere in the background there was the sound of a man's voice raised in song — a song punctuated every now and then by a rhythmic clicking like that of castanets.

"I do believe it's someone playing the spoons, Mr. Brown," exclaimed Mr. Gruber. "I haven't seen that for years."

Paddington, who'd never even heard of anyone playing the spoons before let alone seen it happen, peered around with interest while Mr. Gruber explained how some people, who called themselves "buskers", earned their

living by entertaining the theatre and cinema queues every evening while they were waiting to go in.

To his disappointment the owner of the spoons appeared to be somewhere out of sight round a corner and so rather reluctantly he turned his attention back to the lights.

There were so many different things to see it was difficult to know which to investigate first and he didn't want to run the risk of missing anything, but the Christmas lights themselves seemed very good value indeed. After considering the matter for a moment or two he took off his hat so that the brim wouldn't get in the way and then, holding it out in front of him, he hurried along the pavement after the others with his neck craned back so that he would have a better view.

A little way along the street he was suddenly brought back to earth when he bumped into Mr. Gruber, who'd stopped outside the entrance to the cinema in order to set up his camera on a tripod and make a record of the scene.

Paddington was just staggering back after his collision when to his surprise a man in the front of the near-by queue leaned over and dropped a small, round shiny object into his hat.

"There you are," he said warmly. "Merry Christmas."

"Thank you very much," exclaimed Paddington, looking most surprised. "Merry Christmas to you."

Peering into his hat to see what the man had given him he nearly fell over backwards on to the pavement in astonishment and his eyes grew rounder and rounder as they took in the sight before them.

For inside his hat was not just one, but a whole pile of coins. There were so many, in fact, that the latest addition – whatever it had been – was lost for all time amongst a vast assortment of pennies, threepenny pieces, sixpences; coins of so many different shapes, sizes and values that Paddington soon gave up trying to count them all.

"Is anything the matter, dear?" asked Mrs. Brown, catching sight of the expression on his face. " You look quite . . ." her voice broke off as she too caught a glimpse of the inside of Paddington's hat. "Good gracious!" She put a hand to her mouth. "What *have* you been up to?"

"I haven't been *up* to anything," said Paddington truthfully. Still hardly able to believe his good fortune he gave his hat a shake and several sixpences and a halfpenny fell out through some holes in the side.

"Crikey!" exclaimed Jonathan. "Don't say you've been collecting money from the queue!"

"They must have thought you were with the man playing the spoons," said Judy in alarm.

"Look here," said the man who'd just made the latest contribution to Paddington's collection. "I thought you were a busker."

"A busker!" exclaimed Paddington, giving him a hard stare. "I'm not a busker – I'm a bear!"

"In that case I'd like my sixpence back," said the man sternly. "Collecting money under false pretences."

" 'Ear, 'ear," said a man with a muffler as he pushed his way to the front. "Came round with 'is 'at 'e did. What about my fourpence?"

Mrs. Brown looked round desperately as the murmurings in the front of the queue began to grow and several people farther down the street began pointing in their direction. "Do something, Henry!" she exclaimed.

"*Do something!*" repeated Mr. Brown. "I don't see what *I* can do."

"Well, it was your idea to come up and see the lights in the first place," said Mrs. Brown. "I knew something like this would happen."

"I like that!" exclaimed Mr. Brown indignantly. "It's not my fault." He turned to the queue. "People ought to make sure they know what they are giving their money to before they part with it," he added in a loud voice.

"Came round with 'is 'at 'e did," repeated the man who was wearing the muffler.

"Nonsense!" said Mrs. Bird. "He only happened to be holding it in his paw. It's coming to something if a bear can't walk along a London street with his hat in his paw when he wants to."

"Oh, dear," said Judy. "Look!" She pointed towards the tail end of the queue where another argument appeared to be developing. It was centred around a man dressed in an old raincoat. He was holding an obviously empty hat in one hand while shaking his other fist at a group of people who, in turn, were pointing back up the street towards the Browns.

"Crikey! We're for it now," breathed Jonathan, as the man, having been joined by two stalwart policemen who'd been drawn to the scene by all the noise, turned and began heading in their direction.

"That's 'im! That's 'im!" cried the busker, pointing an accusing finger at Paddington. "Trying to earn an honest bob to buy meself a loaf of bread for Christmas day I was . . . and what 'appens? 'E comes round with 'is 'at and robs me of all me takings!"

The first policeman took out his notebook. "Where do you come from, bear?" he asked sternly.

"Peru," said Paddington promptly. "*Darkest* Peru!"

"Number thirty-two Windsor Gardens," replied Mrs. Brown at the same time.

The policeman looked from one to the other. "No fixed abode," he said ponderously as he licked his pencil.

"No fixed abode!" repeated Mrs. Bird. She took a firm grip of her umbrella and glared at the speaker. "I'll have you know that young bear's abode's been fixed ever since he arrived in this country."

The second policeman viewed Mrs. Bird's umbrella out of the corner of his eye and then glanced round at the rest of the Browns. "I must say they don't look as if they've been working the queues," he said, addressing his colleague.

"Working the queues!" said Mr. Brown indignantly. "We most certainly have been doing nothing of the sort. We came up to show this young bear the lights."

"What about my takings then," interrupted the busker. "' 'Ow do they come to be in 'is 'at?"

"Deliberate it was," shouted the man with the muffler. "Took my fourpence 'e did."

"It certainly wasn't deliberate," said Mr. Gruber, stepping into the breach. "I saw the whole thing through my viewfinder.

"I happened to be taking a photograph at the time, officer," he continued, turning to the first policeman in order to explain the matter, "and I'm quite sure that when it's developed you'll see this young bear is in no way to blame."

Mr. Gruber looked as if he would like to have said a good deal more on the subject but at that moment to everyone's relief a commissionaire appeared at the cinema doors and the queue began to move.

"That's all very well," said the busker. "But what about my takings?

"Two choruses of *Rudolph the Red Nosed Reindeer* I gave

'em on me spoons," he continued plaintively, "and all for nothing."

As the last of the queue disappeared into the cinema and the rest of the crowd began to disperse the first policeman put his notebook away. "It seems to me," he said, turning to his colleague as they made to leave, "if this young bear here gives up his collection everyone'll be happy and we can call it a night. Only look slippy, mind," he continued, addressing himself to Paddington. "Otherwise if certain people are still here when we get back they may find themselves in trouble for causing an obstruction."

Thanking the policeman very much for his advice Paddington began hastily emptying the contents of his hat into the one belonging to the busker.

As the pile of coins cascaded down in a shower of bronze and silver he began to look more and more disappointed. It was difficult to tell exactly how much was in the collection but he felt sure it would have been more than enough to enable Jonathan, Judy and himself to reach their target for the Children's Christmas Party Fund.

"I don't know about no bear's targets," said the busker as Paddington explained what he'd been hoping to do with the money. "I've got me own targets to worry about."

"Never mind, Paddington," said Judy, squeezing his paw. "We've done very well. You never know — something may turn up."

"Tell you what," said the busker, catching sight of the

expression on Paddington's face. "I'll give you a tune on me spoons to cheer you up before you go."

Lifting up his hand he was about to break into the opening bars when to everyone's surprise Mr. Gruber, who had been listening to the conversation with a great deal of interest, suddenly stepped forward. "May I see those spoons a moment?" he asked.

"Certainly, guv'," said the busker, handing them over. "Don't tell me you play 'em as well."

Mr. Gruber shook his head as he took a small spyglass from his pocket and held the spoons up to a near-by lamp so that he could examine them more closely. "You know," he said, "these could be quite valuable. They may even be very rare Georgian silver . . ."

"What!" began the busker, staring open-mouthed at Mr. Gruber. "*My* spoons . . ."

"I have an idea," said Mr. Gruber briskly, silencing the busker with a wave of his hand before he had time to say any more. "If I give you five pounds for this pair of spoons will you let young Mr. Brown keep the collection? After all, he did make it in a way, even if it was an accident."

"Five pounds!" exclaimed the busker, eyeing Mr. Gruber's wallet. "For them spoons? Lor' bless you, sir. Why, 'e can 'ave me 'at as well for that!"

"No, thank you," broke in Mrs. Brown hastily. Paddington's own hat was bad enough at the best of times but from where she was standing it looked as if the busker's might well have matched up to it, give or take a few marmalade stains.

"Tell you what, guv'," said the busker hopefully, as he took Mr. Gruber's five-pound note in exchange for the spoons and began transferring the money back into Paddington's hat. "There's some more where them two came from. 'Ow about . . ."

Mr. Gruber gave him a hard look. "No," he said firmly. "I think these two will do admirably, thank you."

A few minutes later, bidding a rather dazed-looking busker good-bye, the Browns resumed their stroll, with Paddington keeping very much to the outside this time.

"Well," said Mr. Brown, "I'm not quite sure what all

that was about, but it seems to have worked out all right in the end."

"Thirty-seven shillings and fourpence halfpenny," exclaimed Jonathan a few minutes later as he finished counting the money. "That's more than enough to reach our target. I bet they'll be jolly pleased at the hospital."

"I didn't know you were collecting for a children's party," said Mrs. Brown. "You should have said. We could have given you some towards it."

"It was really Paddington's idea," said Judy, giving the paw by her side another squeeze. "Besides, it wouldn't have been the same if you'd given it to us. Not the same at all."

Mr. Brown turned to Mr. Gruber. "Fancy you noticing those spoons," he said. "Isn't it strange how things work out."

"Very strange," agreed Mr. Gruber, taking a sudden interest in some decorations just overhead.

Only Mrs. Bird caught a faint twinkle in his eye – a twinkle not unlike the one she'd noticed when he'd been conducting his deal with the busker, and one moreover which caused her to have certain suspicions on the matter – but wisely she decided it was high time the subject was changed.

"Look," she said, pointing ahead. "There's the Christmas tree in Trafalgar Square. If we hurry we may be in time for the carols."

Mr. Brown gave a sniff. "I'll tell you something else," he said. "I can smell hot chestnuts."

Paddington licked his lips. Although it wasn't long since he'd had his tea all the excitement was beginning to make him feel hungry again. "Hot chestnuts, Mr. Brown," he exclaimed with interest. "I don't think I've ever had any of those before."

The Browns stopped in their tracks and for the second time that day stared at Paddington in amazement.

"You've never had any hot chestnuts?" repeated Mr. Brown.

Paddington shook his head. "Never," he said firmly.

"Well, we can soon alter that," said Mr. Brown, leading the way towards a coke brazier at the side of the road. "Seven large bags, please," he announced to the man who was serving.

"What a good thing I brought my camera," exclaimed Mr. Gruber. "Two firsts in one evening," he continued, as he set up his tripod. "The decorations and now this. I shall have to make some extra copies for your Aunt Lucy in Peru, Mr. Brown. I expect she'll find them most interesting."

Paddington thanked his friend happily through a mouthful of hot chestnuts. In the distance he could still see some decorations in the busy shopping part of London, whilst in front the biggest tree he'd ever seen in his life rose up into the night supporting a myriad of brightly coloured fairy lights, and from somewhere near by the sound of a Christmas carol filled the air. All in all, he thought it had been a lovely evening out and it was nice, not only to think that Christmas Day itself was still to come, but to round things off in such a tasty manner.

"Are you having trouble with your exposures, Mr. Gruber?" he asked hopefully, as he came to the end of his chestnuts.

Mr. Gruber looked up in some surprise. "I only wondered," said Paddington hastily, eyeing the brazier before his friend had time to reply, "because if you are I thought perhaps you'd like me to have another bag just to make sure!"

'There's one thing about bears," said Mrs. Bird,

joining in the laughter which followed Paddington's last remark. "They certainly don't believe in taking any chances!"

Mr. Brown reached into his pocket. "And for once," he said, amid general agreement, "I'm entirely on their side. Seven more bags, please!"

O

BE

ALERT

the new

needs